How to Use This Book

Everything you need to know about Pokémon can be found here in this comprehensive two-volume guide.

This is volume 1 of 2!

The Pokémon in this book are presented in their National Pokédex order. This volume contains numbers 001 to 245, Bulbasaur to Suicune. Volume 2 contains numbers 246 to 491, Larvitar to Darkrai.

If you would like to look up a Pokémon by name, there is an alphabetical index at the end of both volumes.

D0176445

BULBASAUR

Pokémon Data

Seed Pokémon

TYPE	Grass
	Poison
ABILITIES	Overgrow
	. . .
HEIGHT	2′4″
WEIGHT	15.2 lb.

National Pokédex No.
001

Description

As Bulbasaur grows, the plant bulb on its back grows too. When it's very young it draws nutrients from the bulb.

Special Moves

Leech Seed, Vine Whip, PoisonPowder

EVO LUT ION

Bulbasaur → Ivysaur → Venusaur

IVYSAUR

1-49

100-149

150-199

200-249

250-299

300-349

350-399

400-449

450-491

Pokémon Data

Seed Pokémon

TYPE	Grass
	Poison
ABILITIES	Overgrow
	. . .
HEIGHT	3′3″
WEIGHT	28.7 lb.

Description

A sweet smell fills the air when the bud on Ivysaur's back begins to open. But if the bud gets too big, Ivysaur has trouble walking.

Special Moves

Razor Leaf, Sweet Scent, Take Down

National Pokédex No.
002

EVO LUT ION

Bulbasaur   Ivysaur   Venusaur

VENUSAUR

Pokémon Data

Seed Pokémon

TYPE	Grass
	Poison

ABILITIES	Overgrow
	...

HEIGHT	6´7″
WEIGHT	220.5 lb.

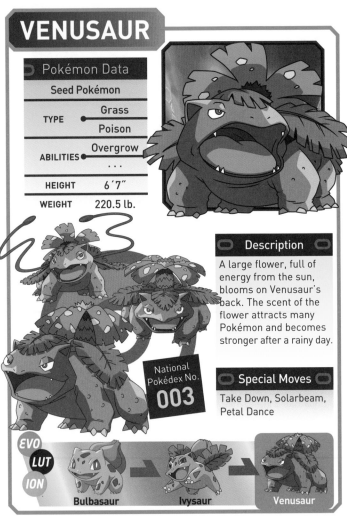

Description

A large flower, full of energy from the sun, blooms on Venusaur's back. The scent of the flower attracts many Pokémon and becomes stronger after a rainy day.

Special Moves

Take Down, Solarbeam, Petal Dance

National Pokédex No.

003

EVO LUT ION

Bulbasaur → Ivysaur → Venusaur

CHARMANDER

Pokémon Data

Lizard Pokémon

TYPE	Fire
	. . .
ABILITIES	Blaze
	. . .
HEIGHT	2'0"
WEIGHT	18.7 lb.

Description

The fire on the tip of Charmander's tail burns from the moment it is born and doesn't go out until its life comes to an end. The flame burns more brightly when it is happy and energetic.

Special Moves

SmokeScreen, Growl, Scratch, Ember

National Pokédex No.

004

EVO LUT ION

Charmander → Charmeleon → Charizard

1-49
50-99
100-149
150-199
200-249
250-299
300-349
350-399
400-449
450-491

CHARMELEON

Pokémon Data

Flame Pokémon

TYPE	Fire ...
ABILITIES	Blaze ...
HEIGHT	3′7″
WEIGHT	41.9 lb.

National Pokédex No.
005

Description

Because of its flame, the temperature of the air around Charmeleon is higher by several degrees.

Special Moves

Fire Fang, Slash, Flamethrower

EVO LUT ION

Charmander → Charmeleon → Charizard

CHARIZARD

Pokémon Data

Flame Pokémon

TYPE	Fire
	Flying
ABILITIES	Blaze
	. . .
HEIGHT	5'7"
WEIGHT	199.5 lb.

National Pokédex No.

006

Description

Charizard can fly almost a mile straight up into the sky and spew scorching flames from its mouth. The more battles it experiences, the hotter its flames become.

Special Moves

Fire Spin, Heat Wave, Flare Blitz

EVO LUT ION

Charmander → Charmeleon → Charizard

49
50-99
100-149
150-199
200-249
250-299
300-349
350-399
400-449
450-491

SQUIRTLE

Pokémon Data

Tiny Turtle Pokémon

TYPE	Water . . .
ABILITIES	Torrent . . .
HEIGHT	1′8″
WEIGHT	19.8 lb.

Description

Squirtle's shell hardens right after it's born. It protects itself by hiding in its shell. Then, at the right moment, it will counterattack with blasts of water.

National Pokédex No.
007

Special Moves

Withdraw, Water Gun, Bite

EVO LUT ION

Squirtle → Wartortle → Blastoise

WARTORTLE

Pokémon Data

Turtle Pokémon

TYPE	Water
	. . .
ABILITIES	Torrent
	. . .
HEIGHT	3'3"
WEIGHT	49.6 lb.

1–49
50–99
100–149
150–199
200–249
250–299
300–349
350–399
400–449
450–491

National Pokédex No.
008

Description

Wartortle lives for a very long time, so its fluffy tail is popular as a symbol for longevity. By moving its ears to adjust its direction, it is able to swim faster underwater.

Special Moves

Rapid Spin, Protect, Water Pulse

EVO LUT ION

Squirtle → Wartortle → Blastoise

BLASTOISE

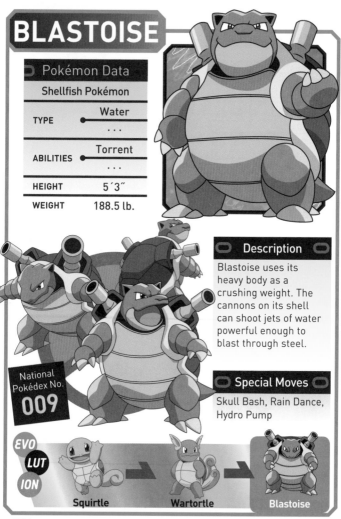

Pokémon Data

Shellfish Pokémon

TYPE	Water . . .
ABILITIES	Torrent . . .
HEIGHT	5´3˝
WEIGHT	188.5 lb.

Description

Blastoise uses its heavy body as a crushing weight. The cannons on its shell can shoot jets of water powerful enough to blast through steel.

Special Moves

Skull Bash, Rain Dance, Hydro Pump

National Pokédex No.
009

EVO LUT ION

Squirtle → Wartortle → Blastoise

CATERPIE

1-49

50-99

100-149

150-199

200-249

250-299

300-349

350-399

400-449

450-491

Pokémon Data

Worm Pokémon

TYPE	Bug ...
ABILITIES	Shield Dust ...
HEIGHT	1′0″
WEIGHT	6.4 lb.

National Pokédex No.

010

Description

Because its feet are actually suction cups Caterpie can easily navigate slopes and walls. The stink that emanates from its red horn can repel its enemies.

Special Moves

Tackle, String Shot

EVO LUT ION

Caterpie   Metapod   Butterfree

METAPOD

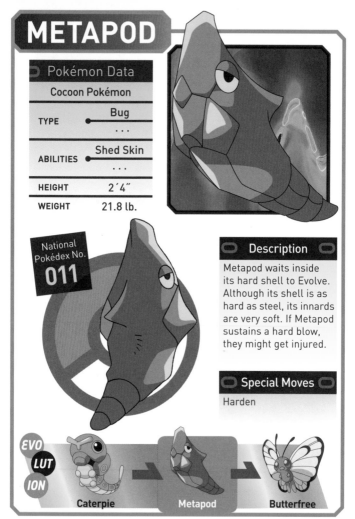

Pokémon Data

Cocoon Pokémon

TYPE	Bug . . .
ABILITIES	Shed Skin . . .
HEIGHT	2´4″
WEIGHT	21.8 lb.

National Pokédex No.
011

Description

Metapod waits inside its hard shell to Evolve. Although its shell is as hard as steel, its innards are very soft. If Metapod sustains a hard blow, they might get injured.

Special Moves

Harden

EVO LUT ION

Caterpie → Metapod → Butterfree

BUTTERFREE

Pokémon Data

Butterfly Pokémon

TYPE	Bug
	Flying
ABILITIES	Compoundeyes
	. . .
HEIGHT	3'7"
WEIGHT	70.5 lb.

National Pokédex No.
012

Description

Because its wings are covered with a fine, water-repellent dust, it can fly even on rainy days. Butterfree loves flower nectar and can locate fields of flowers just by smell.

Special Moves

Gust, Psybeam, Silver Wind, Bug Buzz

EVO LUT ION

Caterpie → Metapod → Butterfree

1-49
50-99
100-149
150-199
200-249
250-299
300-349
350-399
400-449
450-491

WEEDLE

Pokémon Data

Hairy Bug Pokémon

TYPE	Bug
	Poison
ABILITIES	Shield Dust
	...
HEIGHT	1'0"
WEIGHT	7.1 lb.

Description

Weedle lives in forests and grasslands. Every day it eats its body weight in leaves. When attacked, it defends itself using the small poisonous needle atop its head.

Special Moves

Poison Sting, String Shot

National Pokédex No.
013

EVO LUT ION

Weedle → Kakuna → Beedrill

KAKUNA

1-49
50-99
100-149
150-199
200-249
250-299
300-349
350-399
400-449
450-491

Pokémon Data

Cocoon Pokémon

TYPE	Bug
	Poison
ABILITIES	Shed Skin
	. . .
HEIGHT	2′0″
WEIGHT	22.0 lb.

National Pokédex No.
014

Description

Unable to move on its own, Kakuna avoids predators by hiding under leaves and in between branches, where it patiently waits to Evolve.

Special Moves

Harden

EVOLUTION

Weedle	Kakuna	Beedrill

BEEDRILL

Pokémon Data

Poison Bee Pokémon

TYPE	Bug
	Poison
ABILITIES	Swarm
	. . .
HEIGHT	3´3″
WEIGHT	65.0 lb.

National Pokédex No.
015

Description

Beedrill attacks by darting in with great speed, jabbing its opponents with the poisonous needles on its forelimbs and tail, and then quickly flying away.

Special Moves

Twineedle, Pin Missile, Poison Jab

EVO LUT ION

Weedle ▶ Kakuna ▶ Beedrill

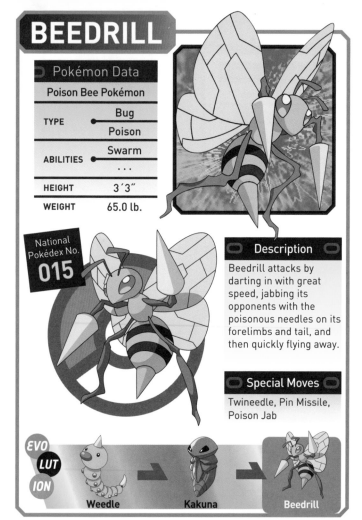

PIDGEY

Pokémon Data

Tiny Bird Pokémon

TYPE	Normal
	Flying
ABILITIES	Keen Eye
	Tangled Feet
HEIGHT	1´0˝
WEIGHT	4.0 lb.

National Pokédex No. **016**

Description

Pidgey lives in forests and grassy thickets, where it hunts small bugs, and tends to shy away from fighting. Although timid, it will defend itself bravely if threatened.

Special Moves

Gust, Quick Attack, Whirlwind

1-49
50-99
100-149
150-199
200-249
250-299
300-349
350-399
400-449
450-491

EVO LUT ION

Pidgey → Pidgeotto → Pidgeot

PIDGEOTTO

Pokémon Data

Bird Pokémon

TYPE	Normal
	Flying
ABILITIES	Keen Eye
	Tangled Feet
HEIGHT	3′7″
WEIGHT	66.1 lb.

National Pokédex No.
017

Description

Pidgeotto constantly patrols its large territory and will attack any enemies that enter it. Its strong claws enable it to fly long distances while carrying its food.

Special Moves

Wing Attack, Tailwind, Mirror Move, Air Slash

EVO LUT ION

Pidgey   Pidgeotto   Pidgeot

PIDGEOT

Pokémon Data

Bird Pokémon

TYPE	Normal
	Flying
ABILITIES	Keen Eye
	Tangled Feet
HEIGHT	4´11″
WEIGHT	87.1 lb.

National Pokédex No.
018

Description

Pidgeot intimidates its opponents by spreading its beautiful wings out wide. With one hard flap, it can create a gust of wind strong enough to snap a large tree.

Special Moves

Whirlwind, FeatherDance, Roost, Mirror Move

1-49
50-99
100-149
150-199
200-249
250-299
300-349
350-399
400-449
450-491

EVO LUT ION

Pidgey Pidgeotto Pidgeot

RATTATA

Pokémon Data

Mouse Pokémon

TYPE	Normal . . .
ABILITIES	Run Away Guts
HEIGHT	1´0˝
WEIGHT	7.7 lb.

National Pokédex No.

019

Description

Rattata can survive practically anywhere and has a tenacious will to live. It keeps its teeth sharp by chewing on hard objects. Its teeth keep growing its entire life.

Special Moves

Bite, Hyper Fang, Sucker Punch

EVO
LUT
ION

Rattata

Raticate

RATICATE

Pokémon Data

Mouse Pokémon

TYPE	Normal
	. . .
ABILITIES	Run Away
	Guts
HEIGHT	2´4˝
WEIGHT	40.8 lb.

National Pokédex No.
020

1-49
50-99
100-149
150-199
200-249
250-299
300-349
350-399
400-449
450-491

Description

Raticate wears down its ever-growing fangs by chewing on hard objects. Its whiskers help it maintain its balance and its back feet are webbed, which enables it to swim.

Special Moves

Crunch, Super Fang, Hyper Fang

EVO LUT ION

  →

Rattata   Raticate

SPEAROW

Pokémon Data

Tiny Bird Pokémon

TYPE	Normal
	Flying
ABILITIES	Keen Eye
	...
HEIGHT	1´0″
WEIGHT	4.4 lb.

National Pokédex No.
021

Description

Spearow must always beat its short wings furiously in order to fly. Nevertheless, it constantly flies about, patrolling its territory.

Special Moves

Fury Attack, Pursuit, Peck, Aerial Ace, Mirror Move

EVOLUTION

Spearow → Fearow

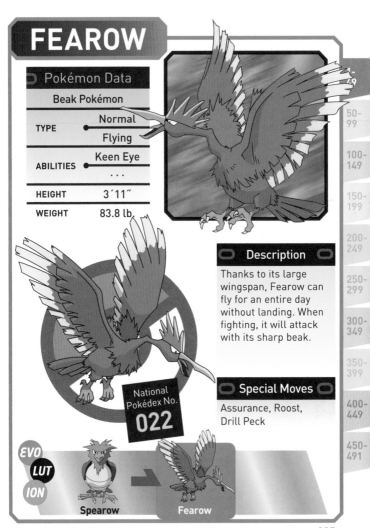

FEAROW

Pokémon Data

Beak Pokémon

TYPE	Normal
	Flying
ABILITIES	Keen Eye
	. . .
HEIGHT	3´11˝
WEIGHT	83.8 lb.

Description

Thanks to its large wingspan, Fearow can fly for an entire day without landing. When fighting, it will attack with its sharp beak.

Special Moves

Assurance, Roost, Drill Peck

National Pokédex No.

022

EVO LUT ION

Spearow → Fearow

49
50-99
100-149
150-199
200-249
250-299
300-349
350-399
400-449
450-491

EKANS

Pokémon Data

Snake Pokémon

TYPE	Poison
	. . .
ABILITIES	Intimidate
	Shed Skin
HEIGHT	6′7″
WEIGHT	15.2 lb.

National Pokédex No.
023

Description

Ekans attacks from behind by hiding its presence while advancing on its prey. It can sense if there is danger in the area by tasting the air with flicks of its tongue.

Special Moves

Bite, Glare, Acid

EVOLUTION

Ekans

Arbok

ARBOK

Pokémon Data

Cobra Pokémon

TYPE	Poison
	. . .
ABILITIES	Intimidate
	Shed Skin
HEIGHT	11′6″
WEIGHT	143.3 lb.

National Pokédex No.
024

Description

Arbok frightens its foes with the scary, face-like pattern on its body. While its opponent is paralyzed with fright, Arbok coils around it and squeezes.

Special Moves

Crunch, Mud Bomb, Gunk Shot

EVO LUT ION

Ekans → Arbok

1-49
50-99
100-149
150-199
200-249
250-299
300-349
350-399
400-449
450-491

PIKACHU

Pokémon Data

Mouse Pokémon

TYPE	Electric
	...
ABILITIES	Static
	...
HEIGHT	1´4″
WEIGHT	13.2 lb.

National
Pokédex No.
025

Description

Pikachu generates and stores electricity in the pouches on its cheeks. When provoked, it can release crackling bolts of electricity from the pouches.

Special Moves

Thunderbolt, Thunder, Double Team

EVO LUT ION

Pichu → Pikachu → Raichu

RAICHU

Pokémon Data

Mouse Pokémon

TYPE	Electric
	...
ABILITIES	Static
	...
HEIGHT	2′7″
WEIGHT	66.1 lb.

National Pokédex No.
026

Description

Raichu often uses Thunderbolt in battle. If too much power builds up in its body, it sticks its tail into the ground and discharges some of the electricity.

Special Moves

Quick Attack, Thunderbolt, ThunderShock

EVO LUT ION

Pichu   Pikachu   Raichu

SANDSHREW

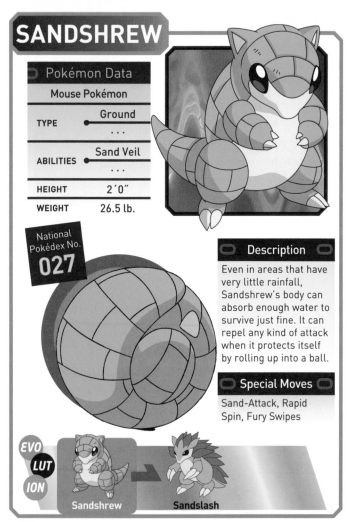

Pokémon Data

Mouse Pokémon

TYPE	Ground
	...
ABILITIES	Sand Veil
	...
HEIGHT	2´0″
WEIGHT	26.5 lb.

National Pokédex No.
027

Description

Even in areas that have very little rainfall, Sandshrew's body can absorb enough water to survive just fine. It can repel any kind of attack when it protects itself by rolling up into a ball.

Special Moves

Sand-Attack, Rapid Spin, Fury Swipes

EVO LUT ION

Sandshrew → Sandslash

SANDSLASH

Pokémon Data

Mouse Pokémon

TYPE	Ground
	. . .
ABILITIES	Sand Veil
	. . .
HEIGHT	3´3˝
WEIGHT	65.0 lb.

National Pokédex No.
028

Description

Sandslash attacks its opponent by rolling up into a ball and body slamming them. It then slashes the stunned enemy with its claws. It can inflict great damage with its spikes.

Special Moves

Rollout, Crush Claw, Sand Tomb

EVO LUT ION

Sandshrew → Sandslash

1–49

50–99

100–149

150–199

200–249

250–299

300–349

350–399

400–449

450–491

NIDORAN ♀

Pokémon Data

Poison Pin Pokémon

TYPE	Poison
	. . .
ABILITIES	Poison Point
	Rivalry
HEIGHT	1´4"
WEIGHT	15.4 lb.

National Pokédex No.
029

Description

Although Nidoran is physically small in size, its poison is still extremely powerful.

Special Moves

Double Kick, Poison Sting, Fury Swipes

EVO LUT ION

Nidoran → Nidorina → Nidoqueen

NIDORINA

Pokémon Data

Poison Pin Pokémon

TYPE	Poison
	. . .
ABILITIES	Poison Point
	Rivalry
HEIGHT	2′7″
WEIGHT	44.1 lb.

1-49

50-99

100-149

150-199

200-249

250-299

300-349

350-399

400-449

450-491

Description

Skilled at scratching and biting, Nidorina confuses its opponent by emitting ultrasonic waves from its mouth. All the spikes on its body stand up when it senses danger.

Special Moves

Helping Hand, Captivate, Toxic Spikes, Crunch

National Pokédex No.
030

EVOLUTION

Nidoran → Nidorina → Nidoqueen

033

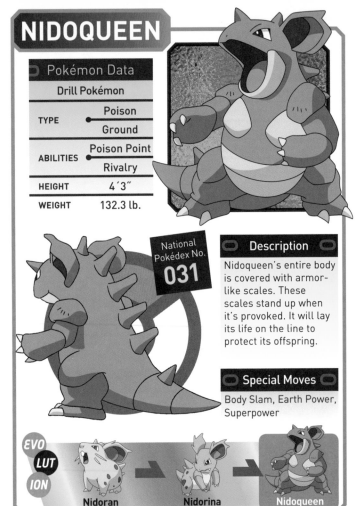

NIDOQUEEN

Pokémon Data

Drill Pokémon

TYPE	Poison
	Ground
ABILITIES	Poison Point
	Rivalry
HEIGHT	4′3″
WEIGHT	132.3 lb.

National Pokédex No.
031

Description

Nidoqueen's entire body is covered with armor-like scales. These scales stand up when it's provoked. It will lay its life on the line to protect its offspring.

Special Moves

Body Slam, Earth Power, Superpower

EVOLUTION

Nidoran → Nidorina → Nidoqueen

NIDORAN♂

Pokémon Data

Poison Pin Pokémon

TYPE	Poison
	. . .
ABILITIES	Poison Point
	Rivalry
HEIGHT	1′8″
WEIGHT	19.8 lb.

Description

The bigger the horn on Nidorino's head, the stronger its poison. It surveys its surroundings by sound, sticking its ears up and flicking them around to catch far-away noises.

National Pokédex No.
032

Special Moves

Focus Energy, Double Kick, Poison Sting

EVOLUTION

Nidoran → Nidorino → Nidoking

1-49
50-99
100-149
150-199
200-249
250-299
300-349
350-399
400-449
450-491

NIDORINO

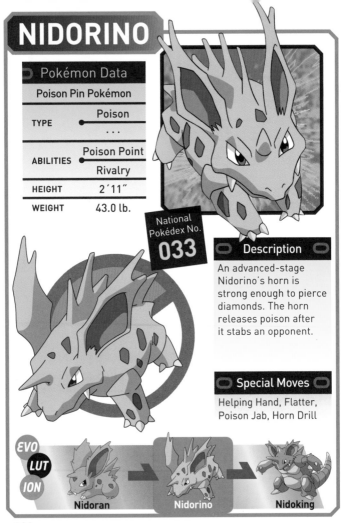

Pokémon Data

Poison Pin Pokémon

TYPE	Poison
	. . .
ABILITIES	Poison Point
	Rivalry
HEIGHT	2´11˝
WEIGHT	43.0 lb.

National Pokédex No.
033

Description

An advanced-stage Nidorino's horn is strong enough to pierce diamonds. The horn releases poison after it stabs an opponent.

Special Moves

Helping Hand, Flatter, Poison Jab, Horn Drill

EVO LUT ION

Nidoran ▸ Nidorino ▸ Nidoking

NIDOKING

Pokémon Data

Drill Pokémon

TYPE	Poison
	Ground
ABILITIES	Poison Point
	Rivalry
HEIGHT	4'7"
WEIGHT	136.7 lb.

150-
199

200-
249

250-
299

300-
349

350-
399

400-
449

450-
491

National
Pokédex No.
034

Description

Nidoking has rock-hard skin, long claws, and a poisonous horn. One strike from its thick tail has enough power to snap a telephone pole in two.

Special Moves

Thrash, Earth Power, Megahorn

EVO LUT ION

Nidoran

Nidorino

Nidoking

CLEFAIRY

Pokémon Data

Fairy Pokémon

TYPE	Normal
	. . .
ABILITIES	Cute Charm
	Magic Guard
HEIGHT	2´0˝
WEIGHT	16.5 lb.

National Pokédex No.
035

Description

Clefairy lives deep in quiet forests, so it is extremely hard to find. It floats by collecting moonlight on the wings on its back. It is a very popular Pokémon because of its cuteness.

Special Moves

Metronome, Moonlight, Meteor Mash

EVO LUT ION

Cleffa

Clefairy

Clefable

CLEFABLE

Pokémon Data

Fairy Pokémon

TYPE	Normal
	. . .

ABILITIES	Cute Charm
	Magic Guard

HEIGHT	4´3˝
WEIGHT	88.2 lb.

National Pokédex No.
036

Description

Clefable is rarely seen by humans. It plays on remote lakes during nights of a full moon. Its hearing is so sharp that it can hear a pin drop over half a mile away.

Special Moves

Sing, Doubleslap, Metronome

EVOLUTION

Cleffa → Clefairy → Clefable

1-49
50-99
100-149
150-199
200-249
250-299
300-349
350-399
400-449
450-491

VULPIX

Pokémon Data

Fox Pokémon

TYPE	Fire
	...
ABILITIES	Flash Fire
	...
HEIGHT	2' 0"
WEIGHT	21.8 lb.

National Pokédex No.
037

Description

When Vulpix is born, it has just one tail. If it is taken very good care of, its tail separates into six new ones. It regulates its body temperature by occasionally releasing some heat.

Special Moves

Will-O-Wisp, Fire Spin, Tail Whip, Roar

EVO LUT ION

Vulpix

Ninetales

NINETALES

Pokémon Data

Fox Pokémon

TYPE	Fire
	...
ABILITIES	Flash Fire
	...
HEIGHT	3′7″
WEIGHT	43.9 lb.

National Pokédex No.
038

1-49

50-99

100-149

150-199

200-249

250-299

300-349

350-399

400-449

450-491

Description

Each of its nine tails holds a divine power, and it can manipulate an opponent's heart with its crimson gaze. Ninetales is said to live for a thousand years.

Special Moves

Ember, Confuse Ray, Safeguard

EVOLUTION

Vulpix → Ninetales

JIGGLYPUFF

Pokémon Data

Balloon Pokémon

TYPE	Normal
	...
ABILITIES	Cute Charm
	...
HEIGHT	1´8˝
WEIGHT	12.1 lb.

National Pokédex No.
039

Description

Jigglypuff lures its opponents close with its big eyes, then puts them to sleep with its lullabies. It sings at the perfect pitch to put each particular opponent to sleep.

Special Moves

Pound, Sing, Defense Curl, Hyper Voice

EVOLUTION

Igglybuff → Jigglypuff → Wigglytuff

WIGGLYTUFF

Pokémon Data

Balloon Pokémon

TYPE	Normal
	. . .
ABILITIES	Cute Charm
	. . .
HEIGHT	3´3˝
WEIGHT	26.5 lb.

National Pokédex No.
040

Description

Wigglytuff can expand to an enormous size by sucking in air. Its air-filled body can float about gently on the breeze. Its fine fur is soft to the touch.

Special Moves

Sing, Defense Curl, Doubleslap

EVO LUT ION

Igglybuff ▸ Jigglypuff ▸ Wigglytuff

1–49
50–99
100–149
150–199
200–249
250–299
300–349
350–399
400–449
450–491

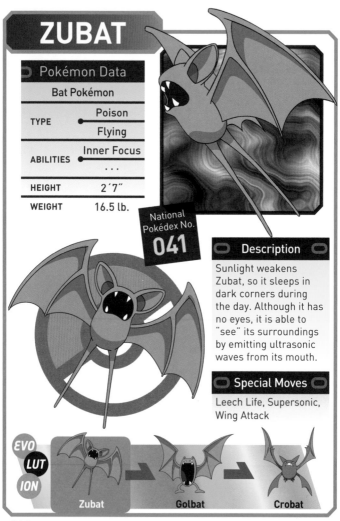

ZUBAT

Pokémon Data

Bat Pokémon

TYPE	Poison
	Flying
ABILITIES	Inner Focus
	. . .
HEIGHT	2′7″
WEIGHT	16.5 lb.

National Pokédex No.
041

Description

Sunlight weakens Zubat, so it sleeps in dark corners during the day. Although it has no eyes, it is able to "see" its surroundings by emitting ultrasonic waves from its mouth.

Special Moves

Leech Life, Supersonic, Wing Attack

EVOLUTION

Zubat → Golbat → Crobat

GOLBAT

Pokémon Data

Bat Pokémon

TYPE	Poison
	Flying
ABILITIES	Inner Focus
	. . .
HEIGHT	5´3˝
WEIGHT	121.3 lb.

Description

Golbat flies around in the dead of night and on moonless nights. It loves the blood of both humans and Pokémon. Once it begins to suck with its four fangs, it will not stop.

National Pokédex No.
042

Special Moves

Mean Look, Poison Fang

EVO LUT ION

Zubat → Golbat → Crobat

1-49
50-99
100-149
150-199
200-249
250-299
300-349
350-399
400-449
450-491

ODDISH

Pokémon Data

Weed Pokémon

TYPE	Grass
	Poison
ABILITIES	Chlorophyll
	. . .
HEIGHT	1′8″
WEIGHT	11.9 lb.

National Pokédex No.
043

Description

During the day, Oddish hardly moves. It roots its feet into the ground and absorbs nutrients from the soil. But at night, it walks around scattering seeds.

Special Moves

Stun Spore, Sleep Powder, Giga Drain

EVO LUT ION

Oddish → Gloom → Bellossom Vileplume

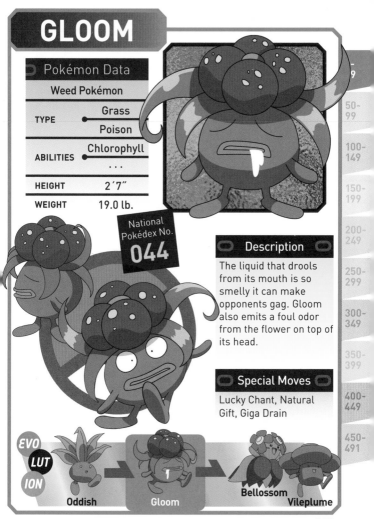

GLOOM

Pokémon Data

Weed Pokémon

TYPE	Grass
	Poison
ABILITIES	Chlorophyll
	. . .
HEIGHT	2′7″
WEIGHT	19.0 lb.

National Pokédex No.
044

Description

The liquid that drools from its mouth is so smelly it can make opponents gag. Gloom also emits a foul odor from the flower on top of its head.

Special Moves

Lucky Chant, Natural Gift, Giga Drain

EVOLUTION

Oddish → Gloom → Bellossom / Vileplume

VILEPLUME

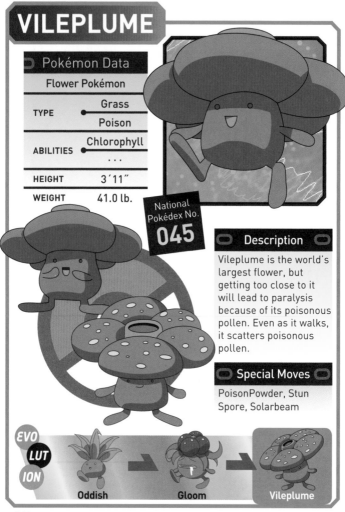

Pokémon Data

Flower Pokémon

TYPE	Grass
	Poison
ABILITIES	Chlorophyll
	. . .
HEIGHT	3´11″
WEIGHT	41.0 lb.

National Pokédex No.
045

Description

Vileplume is the world's largest flower, but getting too close to it will lead to paralysis because of its poisonous pollen. Even as it walks, it scatters poisonous pollen.

Special Moves

PoisonPowder, Stun Spore, Solarbeam

EVO LUT ION

Oddish ▸ Gloom ▸ Vileplume

PARAS

Pokémon Data

Mushroom Pokémon

TYPE	Bug
	Grass
ABILITIES	Effect Spore
	Dry Skin
HEIGHT	1´0˝
WEIGHT	11.9 lb.

National Pokédex No.
046

Description

Paras digs down deep to feed off tree roots. Mushrooms named "to chu kaso" grow on its back.

Special Moves

Leech Life, Stun Spore, Slash

EVO LUT ION

Paras → Parasect

1-49
50-99
00-49
150-199
200-249
250-299
300-349
350-399
400-449
450-491

PARASECT

Pokémon Data

Mushroom Pokémon	
TYPE	Bug
	Grass
ABILITIES	Effect Spore
	Dry Skin
HEIGHT	3'3"
WEIGHT	65.0 lb.

National Pokédex No.

047

Description

Parasect seeks out damp places to live. The mushroom on its back, now larger than Parasect's own body, controls its mind and scatters poison spores wherever Parasect walks.

Special Moves

Stun Spore, Giga Drain, X-Scissor

EVOLUTION

Paras → Parasect

VENONAT

Pokémon Data

Insect Pokémon

TYPE	Bug
	Poison
ABILITIES	Compoundeyes
	Tinted Lens
HEIGHT	3´3˝
WEIGHT	66.1 lb.

National Pokédex No.

048

Description

Venonat gather around sources of light when night falls. Its two big eyes are actually composed of many small eyes. It can move around in the dark by using a kind of radar.

Special Moves

Confusion, PoisonPowder, Signal Beam

1-49

50-99

100-149

150-199

200-249

250-299

300-349

350-399

400-449

450-491

EVO LUT ION

Venonat

Venomoth

VENOMOTH

Pokémon Data

Poison Moth Pokémon

TYPE	Bug
	Poison
ABILITIES	Shield Dust
	Tinted Lens
HEIGHT	4'11"
WEIGHT	27.6 lb.

National Pokédex No.
049

Description

Venomoth scatters toxic powder from its wings as it flies. Poison seeps into the body when the powder makes contact with the target's skin.

Special Moves

Psychic, PoisonPowder, Gust, Stun Spore

EVO LUT ION

Venonat → Venomoth

DIGLETT

Pokémon Data

Mole Pokémon

TYPE	Ground
	. . .
ABILITIES	Sand Veil
	Arena Trap
HEIGHT	0´8˝
WEIGHT	1.8 lb.

National Pokédex No.
050

Description

Diglett lives under the ground, feeding on the roots of plants, and only occasionally pokes its head above ground. Since it lives within the darkness underground, sunlight weakens it.

Special Moves

Magnitude, Sucker Punch, Dig

EVO
LUT
ION

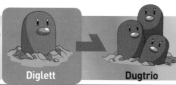

Diglett → Dugtrio

1-49
50-99
100-149
150-199
200-249
250-299
300-349
350-399
400-449
450-491

DUGTRIO

Pokémon Data

	Mole Pokémon
TYPE	Ground . . .
ABILITIES	Sand Veil Arena Trap
HEIGHT	2´4″
WEIGHT	73.4 lb.

National Pokédex No.
051

Description

Dugtrio have great teamwork. No matter how hard the ground is, by working together they can dig more than fifty miles down into the earth.

Special Moves

Sand Tomb, Mud Bomb, Earthquake, Fissure

EVO LUT ION

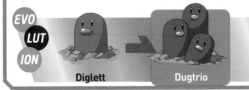

Diglett → Dugtrio

MEOWTH

Pokémon Data

Scratch Cat Pokémon

TYPE	Normal
	. . .
ABILITIES	Pickup
	Technician
HEIGHT	1´4"
WEIGHT	9.3 lb.

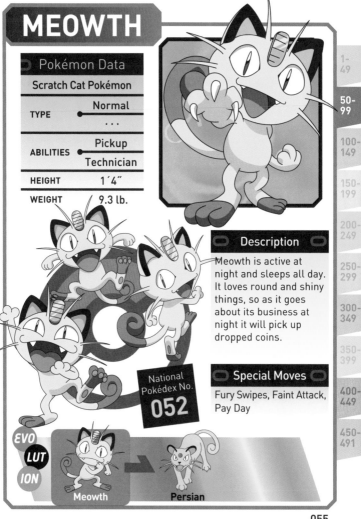

1-49
50-99
100-149
150-199
200-249
250-299
300-349
350-399
400-449
450-491

Description

Meowth is active at night and sleeps all day. It loves round and shiny things, so as it goes about its business at night it will pick up dropped coins.

National Pokédex No.
052

Special Moves

Fury Swipes, Faint Attack, Pay Day

EVO LUT ION

Meowth → Persian

PERSIAN

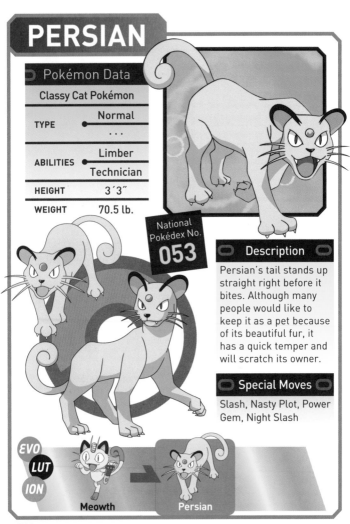

Pokémon Data

Classy Cat Pokémon	
TYPE	Normal . . .
ABILITIES	Limber Technician
HEIGHT	3′3″
WEIGHT	70.5 lb.

National Pokédex No.
053

Description

Persian's tail stands up straight right before it bites. Although many people would like to keep it as a pet because of its beautiful fur, it has a quick temper and will scratch its owner.

Special Moves

Slash, Nasty Plot, Power Gem, Night Slash

EVO LUT ION

Meowth → Persian

PSYDUCK

Pokémon Data

Duck Pokémon

TYPE	Water . . .
ABILITIES	Damp Cloud Nine
HEIGHT	2′7″
WEIGHT	43.2 lb.

National Pokédex No.
054

1– 49

50– 99

100– 149

150– 199

200– 249

250– 299

300– 349

350– 399

400– 449

450– 491

Description

When Psyduck's headache gets bad, it's able to use mysterious psychic powers. But while doing so, it enters a trance-like state, so it doesn't remember anything afterwards.

Special Moves

Water Gun, Disable, Confusion

EVO LUT ION

Psyduck → Golduck

GOLDUCK

Pokémon Data

Duck Pokémon

TYPE	Water
	...
ABILITIES	Damp
	Cloud Nine
HEIGHT	5'7"
WEIGHT	168.9 lb.

National
Pokédex No.
055

Description

The best swimmer of all
Pokémon. Thanks to its
aerodynamic body and
the webbing on its hands
and feet, it can clock
some fierce speeds. It
also has no problem
navigating stormy seas.

Special Moves

Psych Up, Zen Headbutt,
Amnesia

EVO LUT ION

Psyduck ➡ Golduck

MANKEY

Pokémon Data

Pig Monkey Pokémon

TYPE	Fighting
	...
ABILITIES	Vital Spirit
	Anger Point
HEIGHT	1´8˝
WEIGHT	61.7 lb.

National Pokédex No.
056

Description

Mankey live in trees. If even just one member of the troop gets angry—and even the smallest thing causes them to get angry—they'll all start fighting.

Special Moves

Karate Chop, Seismic Toss, Thrash

EVO LUT ION

Mankey → Primeape

50-99
100-149
150-199
200-249
250-299
300-349
350-399
400-449
450-491

PRIMEAPE

Pokémon Data

Pig Monkey Pokémon

TYPE	Fighting . . .
ABILITIES	Vital Spirit Anger Point
HEIGHT	3´3˝
WEIGHT	70.5 lb.

National Pokédex No.

057

Description

For some reason, Primeape is always angry. Even just making eye contact will infuriate it. It will pursue anything that runs away from it. And if it loses, it gets even madder.

Special Moves

Rage, Cross Chop, Thrash

EVO LUT ION

Mankey → Primeape

GROWLITHE

Pokémon Data

Puppy Pokémon

TYPE	Fire
	...
ABILITIES	Intimidate
	Flash Fire
HEIGHT	2′4″
WEIGHT	41.9 lb.

National Pokédex No.

058

Description

Growlithe is very protective of its territory and will growl and snap if it feels threatened. It's very obedient to its Trainer; it won't take even a single step unless ordered.

Special Moves

Ember, Roar, Flame Wheel, Take Down

EVO LUT ION

Growlithe → Arcanine

1-49
50-99
100-149
150-199
200-249
250-299
300-349
350-399
400-449
450-491

ARCANINE

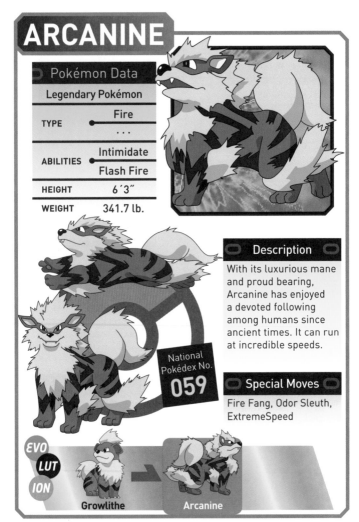

Pokémon Data

Legendary Pokémon

TYPE	Fire
	. . .
ABILITIES	Intimidate
	Flash Fire
HEIGHT	6′3″
WEIGHT	341.7 lb.

National Pokédex No. **059**

Description

With its luxurious mane and proud bearing, Arcanine has enjoyed a devoted following among humans since ancient times. It can run at incredible speeds.

Special Moves

Fire Fang, Odor Sleuth, ExtremeSpeed

EVO LUT ION

Growlithe → Arcanine

POLIWAG

Pokémon Data

Tadpole Pokémon

TYPE	Water
	. . .
ABILITIES	Water Absorb
	Damp
HEIGHT	2′0″
WEIGHT	27.3 lb.

National Pokédex No.
060

Description

Because Poliwag has just grown its feet, it can't walk very well. The spiral pattern on its belly is actually part of its intestines, which are visible through its thin skin.

Special Moves

Hypnosis, Water Gun, Rain Dance

1-49
50-99
100-149
150-199
200-249
250-299
300-349
350-399
400-449
450-491

EVO LUT ION

Poliwag   Poliwhirl   Politoed   Poliwrath

POLIWHIRL

Pokémon Data

Tadpole Pokémon

TYPE	Water
	...
ABILITIES	Water Absorb
	Damp
HEIGHT	3'3"
WEIGHT	44.1 lb.

National Pokédex No.
061

Description

Poliwhirl can live both on land and in water. While on land, it keeps its body moist with a slimy film. Staring at the spiral pattern on its belly can cause one to become drowsy.

Special Moves

Body Slam, Belly Drum, Wake-Up Slap

EVO LUT ION

Poliwag → Poliwhirl → Politoed Poliwrath

POLIWRATH

Pokémon Data

Tadpole Pokémon	
TYPE	Water
	Fighting
ABILITIES	Water Absorb
	Damp
HEIGHT	4′3″
WEIGHT	119.0 lb.

National Pokédex No.

062

1-49

50-99

100-149

150-199

200-249

250-299

300-349

350-399

400-449

450-491

Description

Poliwrath is very good at swimming and can use many different strokes. It's very strong and muscular, so it can swim across wide oceans without rest.

Special Moves

Submission, Dynamic Punch, Mind Reader

EVO LUT ION

Poliwag ➤ Poliwhirl ➤ Poliwrath

ABRA

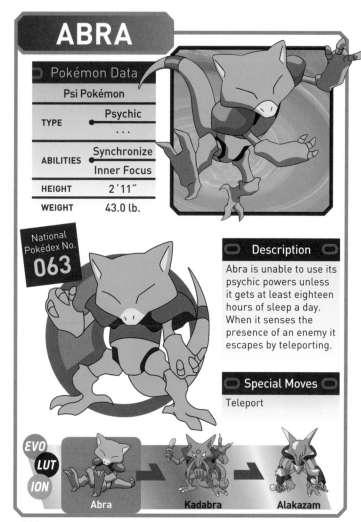

Pokémon Data

Psi Pokémon

TYPE	Psychic
	. . .
ABILITIES	Synchronize
	Inner Focus
HEIGHT	2′11″
WEIGHT	43.0 lb.

National Pokédex No.
063

Description

Abra is unable to use its psychic powers unless it gets at least eighteen hours of sleep a day. When it senses the presence of an enemy it escapes by teleporting.

Special Moves

Teleport

EVOLUTION

Abra → Kadabra → Alakazam

KADABRA

Pokémon Data

Psi Pokémon	
TYPE	Psychic
	. . .
ABILITIES	Synchronize
	Inner Focus
HEIGHT	4´3˝
WEIGHT	124.6 lb.

National Pokédex No.
064

Description

Whenever Kadabra uses its psychic powers, it unleashes a surge of powerful alpha waves. The spoon in its hand is said to strengthen the power of the alpha waves.

Special Moves

Psybeam, Reflect, Psycho Cut

1-49
50-99
100-149
150-199
200-249
250-299
300-349
350-399
400-449
450-491

EVO LUT ION

Abra — Kadabra — Alakazam

ALAKAZAM

Pokémon Data

Psi Pokémon

TYPE	Psychic
	. . .
ABILITIES	Synchronize
	Inner Focus
HEIGHT	4'11"
WEIGHT	105.8 lb.

National Pokédex No.
065

Description

Alakazam's IQ measures above 5,000 and it has mastered a multitude of ESP techniques. It remembers everything that has happened to it starting from the moment of its birth.

Special Moves

Calm Mind, Psychic, Future Sight

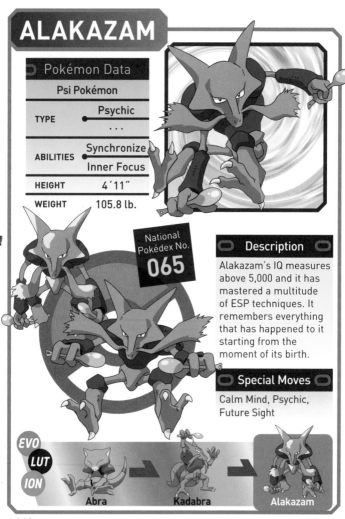

EVOLUTION

Abra → Kadabra → Alakazam

MACHOP

Pokémon Data

Superpower Pokémon

TYPE	Fighting
	. . .
ABILITIES	Guts
	No Guard
HEIGHT	2′7″
WEIGHT	43.0 lb.

Description

Machop works out by lifting Graveler. Some Machop travel the world in order to hone their fighting skills.

Special Moves

Focus Energy, Karate Chop, Foresight

National Pokédex No.
066

EVO LUT ION

Machop   Machoke   Machamp

1-49
50-99
100-149
150-199
200-249
250-299
300-349
350-399
400-449
450-491

MACHOKE

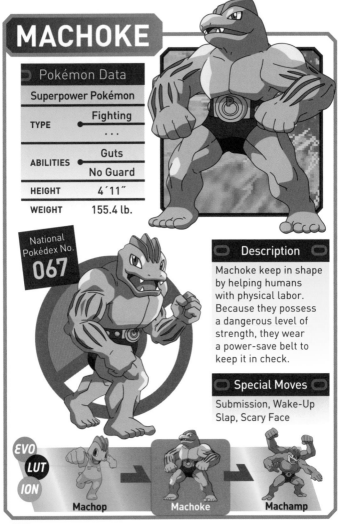

Pokémon Data

Superpower Pokémon

TYPE	Fighting
	...
ABILITIES	Guts
	No Guard
HEIGHT	4'11"
WEIGHT	155.4 lb.

National Pokédex No.
067

Description

Machoke keep in shape by helping humans with physical labor. Because they possess a dangerous level of strength, they wear a power-save belt to keep it in check.

Special Moves

Submission, Wake-Up Slap, Scary Face

EVOLUTION

Machop ▶ Machoke ▶ Machamp

MACHAMP

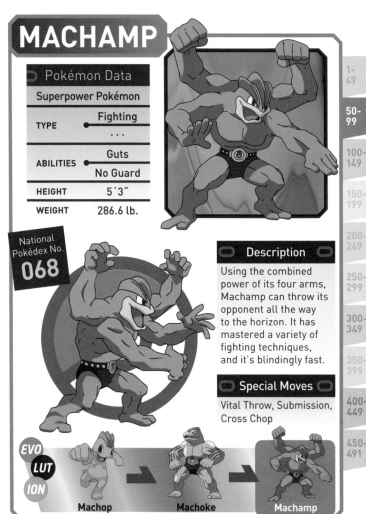

Pokémon Data

Superpower Pokémon

TYPE	Fighting
	. . .
ABILITIES	Guts
	No Guard
HEIGHT	5′3″
WEIGHT	286.6 lb.

National Pokédex No.
068

Description

Using the combined power of its four arms, Machamp can throw its opponent all the way to the horizon. It has mastered a variety of fighting techniques, and it's blindingly fast.

Special Moves

Vital Throw, Submission, Cross Chop

EVO LUT ION

Machop ▶ Machoke ▶ Machamp

1-49
50-99
100-149
150-199
200-249
250-299
300-349
350-399
400-449
450-491

BELLSPROUT

Pokémon Data

Flower Pokémon	
TYPE	Grass
	Poison
ABILITIES	Chlorophyll
	. . .
HEIGHT	2′4″
WEIGHT	8.8 lb.

National Pokédex No. **069**

Description

Bellsprout loves damp places where it can suck up water from the ground through its foot roots. It captures opponents by snaring them with its vines.

Special Moves

PoisonPowder, Sleep Powder, Stun Spore, Vine Whip

EVOLUTION

Bellsprout

Weepinbell

Victreebel

WEEPINBELL

Pokémon Data

Flycatcher Pokémon

TYPE	Grass
	Poison
ABILITIES	Chlorophyll
	...
HEIGHT	3´3˝
WEIGHT	14.1 lb.

National Pokédex No.
070

Description

Weepinbell captures prey that wander near it by dusting them with PoisonPowder. It can shoot out razor-sharp leaves, and it can spit an acid-like liquid from its mouth.

Special Moves

Odor Sleuth, Mud-Slap, Powder Snow, Endure

EVOLUTION

Bellsprout ▸ **Weepinbell** ▸ **Victreebel**

1-49
50-99
100-149
150-199
200-249
250-299
300-349
350-399
400-449
450-491

VICTREEBEL

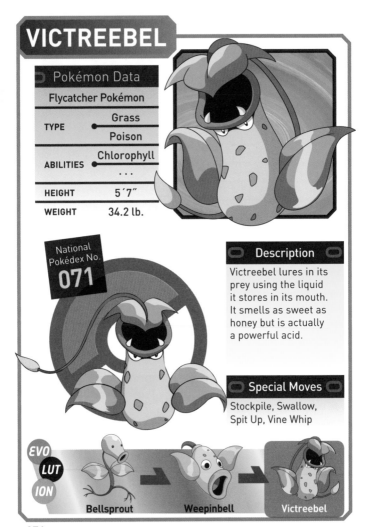

Pokémon Data

Flycatcher Pokémon

TYPE	Grass
	Poison
ABILITIES	Chlorophyll
	. . .
HEIGHT	5´7˝
WEIGHT	34.2 lb.

National Pokédex No.
071

Description

Victreebel lures in its prey using the liquid it stores in its mouth. It smells as sweet as honey but is actually a powerful acid.

Special Moves

Stockpile, Swallow, Spit Up, Vine Whip

EVOLUTION

Bellsprout ➤ Weepinbell ➤ Victreebel

TENTACOOL

Pokémon Data

Jellyfish Pokémon	
TYPE	Water
	Poison
ABILITIES	Clear Body
	Liquid Ooze
HEIGHT	2′11″
WEIGHT	100.3 lb.

National Pokédex No.
072

Description

Because Tentacool's body is made mostly of water it will shrivel up if it's taken out of the ocean. It can emit mysterious energy beams from its crystalline eyes.

Special Moves

Poison Sting, Acid, Toxic Spikes, BubbleBeam

EVO LUT ION

Tentacool → Tentacruel

1-49
50-99
100-149
150-199
200-249
250-299
300-349
350-399
400-449
450-491

TENTACRUEL

Pokémon Data

Jellyfish Pokémon

TYPE	Water
	Poison
ABILITIES	Clear Body
	Liquid Ooze
HEIGHT	5′3″
WEIGHT	121.3 lb.

National Pokédex No.

073

Description

It captures its prey using its extendable tentacles and then weakens it with poison. When it senses danger it transmits the information to its mates by using the red orbs on its head.

Special Moves

Poison Jab, Hydro Pump, Barrier

EVO LUT ION

Tentacool

Tentacruel

GEODUDE

Pokémon Data

Rock Pokémon

TYPE	Rock
	Ground
ABILITIES	Rock Head
	Sturdy
HEIGHT	1′4″
WEIGHT	44.1 lb.

National Pokédex No.
074

Description

It rolls along slopes in search of food. When it sleeps, it buries half its body in the ground. The older it gets, the more its edges are worn away, making its body round and smooth.

Special Moves

Defense Curl, Mud Sport, Rollout, Selfdestruct

EVO
LUT
ION

Geodude → Graveler → Golem

1-49
50-99
100-149
150-199
200-249
250-299
300-349
350-399
400-449
450-491

GRAVELER

Pokémon Data

Rock Pokémon	
TYPE	Rock
	Ground
ABILITIES	Rock Head
	Sturdy
HEIGHT	3′3″
WEIGHT	231.5 lb.

National Pokédex No.
075

Description

Graveler grows by eating a ton of rocks a day. It especially loves rocks with moss on them. It eats rocks as it climbs hills; once it reaches the top, it rolls down to the bottom again.

Special Moves

Magnitude, Rollout, Double-Edge

EVO LUT ION

Geodude → Graveler → Golem

GOLEM

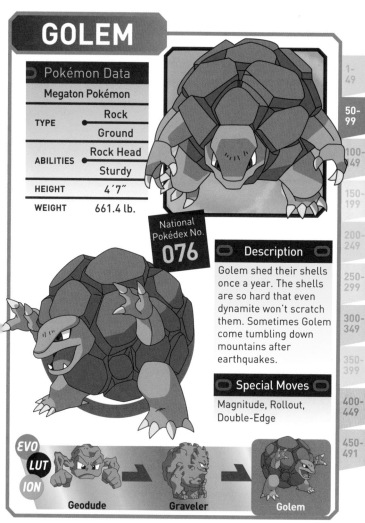

Pokémon Data

Megaton Pokémon

TYPE	Rock
	Ground
ABILITIES	Rock Head
	Sturdy
HEIGHT	4'7"
WEIGHT	661.4 lb.

National Pokédex No.
076

Description

Golem shed their shells once a year. The shells are so hard that even dynamite won't scratch them. Sometimes Golem come tumbling down mountains after earthquakes.

Special Moves

Magnitude, Rollout, Double-Edge

EVOLUTION

Geodude → Graveler → Golem

1–49
50–99
100–149
150–199
200–249
250–299
300–349
350–399
400–449
450–491

PONYTA

Pokémon Data

Fire Horse Pokémon	
TYPE	Fire
	...
ABILITIES	Run Away
	Flash Fire
HEIGHT	3´3″
WEIGHT	66.1 lb.

National
Pokédex No.
077

Description

Ponyta's legs are extremely strong: it can trample under its hooves anything that gets in its way. Within an hour of being born, its tail and mane of flames grow out.

Special Moves

Ember, Stomp, Fire Spin, Take Down

**EVO
LUT
ION**

Ponyta

Rapidash

RAPIDASH

Pokémon Data

Fire Horse Pokémon

TYPE	Fire
	. . .
ABILITIES	Run Away
	Flash Fire
HEIGHT	5'7"
WEIGHT	209.4 lb.

National Pokédex No.
078

Description

Rapidash's mane forms a roaring blaze as it runs. In a mere ten steps, it can achieve maximum speed. When it sees something that moves fast, it will want to race against it.

Special Moves

Fire Blast, Fury Attack, Flare Blitz

EVO LUT ION

Ponyta ➡ Rapidash

SLOWPOKE

Pokémon Data

Dopey Pokémon	
TYPE	Water
	Psychic
ABILITIES	Oblivious
	Own Tempo
HEIGHT	3'11"
WEIGHT	79.4 lb.

National Pokédex No.
079

Description

Although it moves very slowly, Slowpoke is skilled at fishing using its tail. Since it's oblivious to almost everything, it doesn't feel any pain, even when its tail is bitten.

Special Moves

Curse, Confusion, Water Gun, Yawn

EVOLUTION

Slowpoke → Slowbro → Slowking

SLOWBRO

Pokémon Data

Hermit Crab Pokémon

TYPE	Water
	Psychic
ABILITIES	Oblivious
	Own Tempo
HEIGHT	5´3"
WEIGHT	173.1 lb.

National Pokédex No. **080**

Description

Slowbro Evolved from a Slowpoke when it was bitten by a Shellder while searching for food. Whenever the Shellder bites down hard on its tail, Slowbro becomes inspired.

Special Moves

Amnesia, Psychic, Psych Up

1- 49

50- 99

100- 149

150- 199

200- 249

250- 299

300- 349

350- 399

400- 449

450- 491

EVO LUT ION

Slowpoke

Slowbro

Slowking

MAGNEMITE

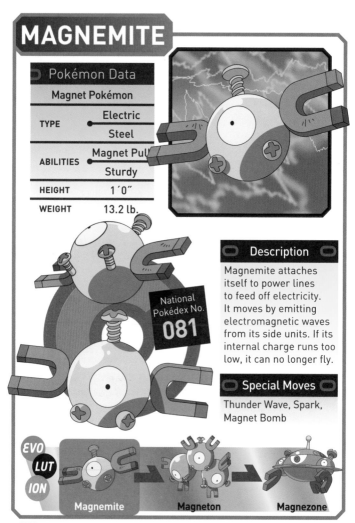

Pokémon Data

Magnet Pokémon	
TYPE	Electric
	Steel
ABILITIES	Magnet Pull
	Sturdy
HEIGHT	1′0″
WEIGHT	13.2 lb.

National Pokédex No. **081**

Description

Magnemite attaches itself to power lines to feed off electricity. It moves by emitting electromagnetic waves from its side units. If its internal charge runs too low, it can no longer fly.

Special Moves

Thunder Wave, Spark, Magnet Bomb

EVOLUTION

Magnemite ➤ Magneton ➤ Magnezone

MAGNETON

Pokémon Data

Magnet Pokémon

TYPE	Electric
	Steel
ABILITIES	Magnet Pull
	Sturdy
HEIGHT	3´3˝
WEIGHT	132.3 lb.

National Pokédex No.

082

Description

Magneton is made up of three Magnemite stuck together. It can create a powerful magnetic force field and discharge a voltage high enough to cause most machinery to malfunction.

Special Moves

Discharge, Mirror Shot, Magnet Bomb

1-49
50-99
100-149
150-199
200-249
250-299
300-349
350-399
400-449
450-491

EVOLUTION

Magnemite → Magneton → Magnezone

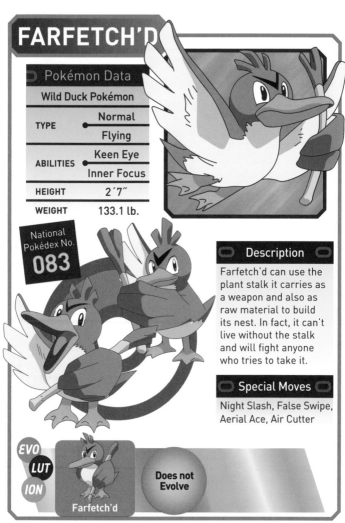

FARFETCH'D

Pokémon Data

Wild Duck Pokémon

TYPE	Normal
	Flying
ABILITIES	Keen Eye
	Inner Focus
HEIGHT	2′7″
WEIGHT	133.1 lb.

National Pokédex No.

083

Description

Farfetch'd can use the plant stalk it carries as a weapon and also as raw material to build its nest. In fact, it can't live without the stalk and will fight anyone who tries to take it.

Special Moves

Night Slash, False Swipe, Aerial Ace, Air Cutter

EVO LUT ION

Farfetch'd

Does not Evolve

DODUO

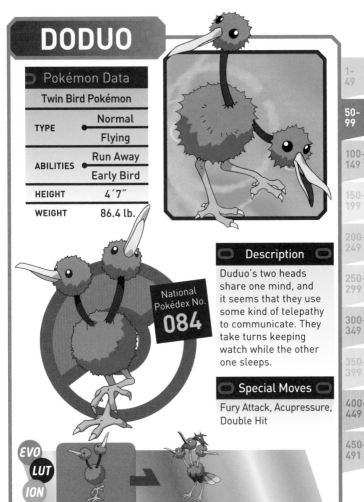

Pokémon Data

Twin Bird Pokémon

TYPE	Normal
	Flying
ABILITIES	Run Away
	Early Bird
HEIGHT	4'7"
WEIGHT	86.4 lb.

National Pokédex No.
084

Description

Duduo's two heads share one mind, and it seems that they use some kind of telepathy to communicate. They take turns keeping watch while the other one sleeps.

Special Moves

Fury Attack, Acupressure, Double Hit

EVO LUT ION

Doduo ➜ Dodrio

1-49
50-99
100-149
150-199
200-249
250-299
300-349
350-399
400-449
450-491

DODRIO

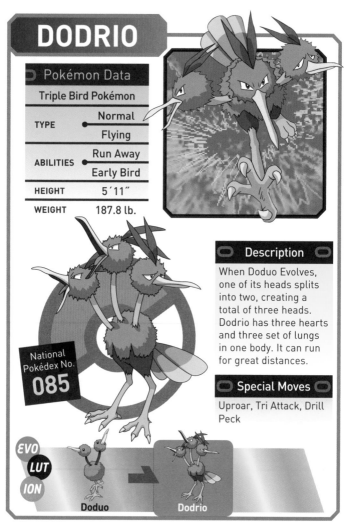

Pokémon Data

Triple Bird Pokémon

TYPE	Normal
	Flying
ABILITIES	Run Away
	Early Bird
HEIGHT	5′11″
WEIGHT	187.8 lb.

National Pokédex No.
085

Description

When Doduo Evolves, one of its heads splits into two, creating a total of three heads. Dodrio has three hearts and three set of lungs in one body. It can run for great distances.

Special Moves

Uproar, Tri Attack, Drill Peck

EVO LUT ION

Doduo → Dodrio

SEEL

Pokémon Data

Sea Lion Pokémon

TYPE	Water
	...
ABILITIES	Thick Fat
	Hydration
HEIGHT	3´7˝
WEIGHT	198.4 lb.

National Pokédex No.
086

Description

Seel lives on icebergs. The horn on its head is extremely hard and it uses this to break the ice as it swims. Its thick skin and white fur keep it comfortable in cold temperatures.

Special Moves

Icy Wind, Aurora Beam, Brine

EVO LUT ION

Seel   Dewgong

49

50-99

100-149

150-199

200-249

250-299

300-349

350-399

400-449

450-491

DEWGONG

Pokémon Data

Sea Lion Pokémon	
TYPE	Water
	Ice
ABILITIES	Thick Fat
	Hydration
HEIGHT	5′7″
WEIGHT	264.6 lb.

National Pokédex No.
087

Description

Dewgong stores up heat in its body and becomes more active the colder it gets. Because the fur on its entire body is pure white, it is camouflaged well from enemies in the snow.

Special Moves

Dive, Aqua Tail, Safeguard

EVO LUT ION

Seel

Dewgong

GRIMER

Pokémon Data

Sludge Pokémon	
TYPE	Poison
	. . .
ABILITIES	Stench
	Sticky Hold
HEIGHT	2´11″
WEIGHT	66.1 lb.

National Pokédex No.
088

Description

Grimer was born when sludge in a dirty stream was exposed to lunar x-rays. It leaks bacteria-laden ooze from every pore on its body and can pass through even the narrowest of openings.

Special Moves

Poison Gas, Minimize, Sludge

EVO LUT ION

Grimer   Muk

1-49
50-99
100-149
150-199
200-249
250-299
300-349
350-399
400-449
450-491

MUK

Pokémon Data

Sludge Pokémon

TYPE	Poison
	. . .
ABILITIES	Stench
	Sticky Hold
HEIGHT	3´11˝
WEIGHT	66.1 lb.

National Pokédex No.
089

Description

Muk loves to eat filthy things. A deadly, poisonous and horribly noxious fluid oozes from its body. The fluid is so powerful that it kills plants and trees on contact.

Special Moves

Sludge Bomb, Gunk Shot, Acid Armor

EVO LUT ION

Grimer → Muk

SHELLDER

Pokémon Data

Bivalve Pokémon

TYPE	Water
	. . .

ABILITIES	Shell Armor
	Skill Link

HEIGHT	1′0″
WEIGHT	8.8 lb.

National
Pokédex No.
090

Description

Shellder swims by rapidly opening and closing its two shells, which are harder than diamonds. Its large tongue is always sticking out.

Special Moves

Icicle Spear, Protect, Clamp

EVO
LUT
ION

Shellder   Cloyster

1-
49

50-
99

100-
149

150-
199

200-
249

250-
299

300-
349

350-
399

400-
449

450-
491

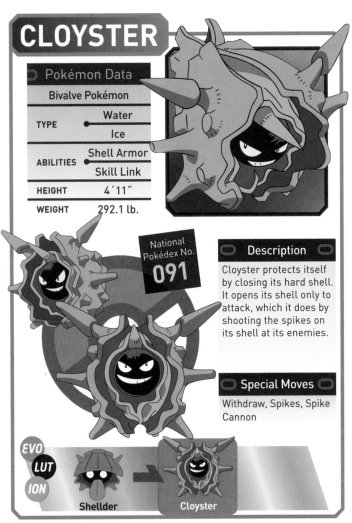

CLOYSTER

Pokémon Data

Bivalve Pokémon

TYPE	Water
	Ice
ABILITIES	Shell Armor
	Skill Link
HEIGHT	4´11˝
WEIGHT	292.1 lb.

National Pokédex No.
091

Description

Cloyster protects itself by closing its hard shell. It opens its shell only to attack, which it does by shooting the spikes on its shell at its enemies.

Special Moves

Withdraw, Spikes, Spike Cannon

EVO LUT ION

Shellder → Cloyster

GASTLY

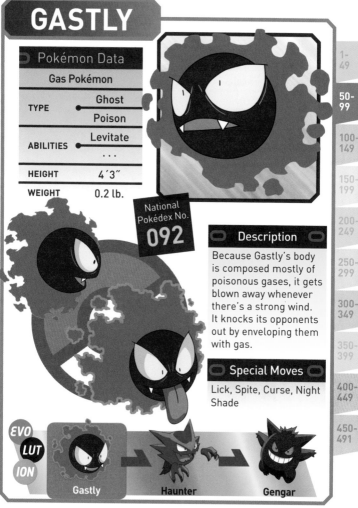

Pokémon Data

Gas Pokémon

TYPE	Ghost
	Poison
ABILITIES	Levitate
	...
HEIGHT	4'3"
WEIGHT	0.2 lb.

National Pokédex No.
092

Description

Because Gastly's body is composed mostly of poisonous gases, it gets blown away whenever there's a strong wind. It knocks its opponents out by enveloping them with gas.

Special Moves

Lick, Spite, Curse, Night Shade

EVOLUTION

Gastly → Haunter → Gengar

1-49
50-99
100-149
150-199
200-249
250-299
300-349
350-399
400-449
450-491

HAUNTER

Pokémon Data

Gas Pokémon

TYPE	Ghost
	Poison
ABILITIES	Levitate
	. . .
HEIGHT	5´3˝
WEIGHT	0.2 lb.

National Pokédex No.
093

Description

Haunter can move through any substance. It hides in dark shadows and watches and waits. It absorbs life force by licking its prey with its gaseous tongue.

Special Moves

Payback, Destiny Bond, Shadow Punch

EVO LUT ION

Gastly

Haunter

Gengar

GENGAR

Pokémon Data

Shadow Pokémon

TYPE	Ghost
	Poison
ABILITIES	Levitate
	...
HEIGHT	4′11″
WEIGHT	89.3 lb.

National Pokédex No.
094

Description

Gengar lurks in dark corners. On the nights of a full moon, when your shadow moves on its own and starts laughing, Gengar is most likely behind it.

Special Moves

Dream Eater, Dark Pulse, Destiny Bond, Nightmare

EVOLUTION

Gastly ➤ Haunter ➤ Gengar

1-49
50-99
100-149
150-199
200-249
250-299
300-349
350-399
400-449
450-491

ONIX

Pokémon Data

Rock Snake Pokémon

TYPE	Rock
	Ground
ABILITIES	Rock Head
	Sturdy
HEIGHT	28´10˝
WEIGHT	463.0 lb.

National Pokédex No.

095

Description

Onix lives underground. As it grows, its body gradually becomes darker and harder, until it's tough as diamonds. It can move as fast as fifty miles per hour.

Special Moves

Bind, Rock Throw, Rock Tomb

EVO LUT ION

Onix

Steelix

DROWZEE

Pokémon Data

Hypnosis Pokémon

TYPE	Psychic . . .
ABILITIES	Insomnia Forewarn
HEIGHT	3´3″
WEIGHT	71.4 lb.

1-
49

50-
99

100-
149

150-
199

200-
249

250-
299

300-
349

350-
399

400-
449

450-
491

Description

Drowzee eats human dreams. If it eats too many nightmares, though, it can get a stomachache. It uses its nose to sniff out what a person is dreaming.

National Pokédex No.
096

Special Moves

Hypnosis, Confusion, Psybeam

EVO LUT ION

Drowzee → Hypno

HYPNO

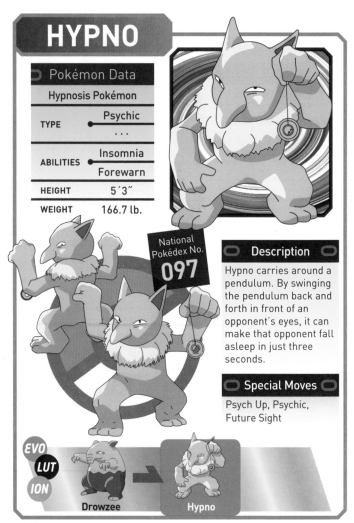

Pokémon Data

Hypnosis Pokémon

TYPE	Psychic
	...
ABILITIES	Insomnia
	Forewarn
HEIGHT	5′3″
WEIGHT	166.7 lb.

National Pokédex No.

097

Description

Hypno carries around a pendulum. By swinging the pendulum back and forth in front of an opponent's eyes, it can make that opponent fall asleep in just three seconds.

Special Moves

Psych Up, Psychic, Future Sight

EVO LUT ION

Drowzee → Hypno

KRABBY

Pokémon Data

River Crab Pokémon

TYPE	Water
	. . .
ABILITIES	Hyper Cutter
	Shell Armor
HEIGHT	1′4″
WEIGHT	14.3 lb.

National Pokédex No.

098

Description

Krabby uses its claws to keep its balance as it scuttles along. Even if it loses a claw during battle, it can quickly grow a new one.

Special Moves

Harden, BubbleBeam, Metal Claw

EVO LUT ION

Krabby → Kingler

1–49

50–99

100–149

150–199

200–249

250–299

300–349

350–399

400–449

450–491

KINGLER

Pokémon Data

Pincer Pokémon

TYPE	Water . . .
ABILITIES	Hyper Cutter Shell Armor
HEIGHT	4′3″
WEIGHT	132.3 lb.

National Pokédex No.
099

Description

Its enormous scissor claw can exert force equivalent to 10,000 horsepower. But because the claw is so heavy, Kingler has a hard time being accurate with it.

Special Moves

Guillotine, Brine, Crabhammer

EVOLUTION

Krabby → Kingler

VOLTORB

Pokémon Data

Ball Pokémon

TYPE	Electric
	. . .
ABILITIES	Soundproof
	Static
HEIGHT	1´8˝
WEIGHT	22.9 lb.

National Pokédex No.
100

Description

Voltorb are thought to be created when Pokéballs are exposed to very strong electrical fields. Touching one accidentally might result in an electric shock.

Special Moves

Spark, Charge Beam, Selfdestruct

EVO
LUT
ION

Voltorb → Electrode

1-49

50-99

100-149

150-199

200-249

250-299

300-349

350-399

400-449

450-491

ELECTRODE

Pokémon Data

Ball Pokémon	
TYPE	Electric
	...
ABILITIES	Soundproof
	Static
HEIGHT	3´11˝
WEIGHT	146.8 lb.

National Pokédex No.
101

Description

Electrode consumes static electricity and also eats the electricity at power plants, which causes headaches for humans.

Special Moves

Magnet Rise, Explosion, Charge Beam

EVO LUT ION

Voltorb

Electrode

EXEGGCUTE

Pokémon Data

Egg Pokémon

TYPE	Grass
	Psychic
ABILITIES	Chlorophyll
	. . .
HEIGHT	1′4″
WEIGHT	5.5 lb.

National Pokédex No.
102

Description

Although they look like eggs, Exeggcute are actually more like plant seeds. They can communicate with others of their kind by telepathy.

Special Moves

Barrage, Reflect, Bullet Seed

EVO LUT ION

Exeggcute

Exeggutor

1-49
50-99
100-149
150-199
200-249
250-299
300-349
350-399
400-449
450-491

EXEGGUTOR

Pokémon Data

Coconut Pokémon

TYPE	Grass
	Psychic

ABILITIES	Chlorophyll
	...

HEIGHT	6′7″
WEIGHT	264.6 lb.

National Pokédex No.
103

Description

Exeggutor is sometimes called "The Walking Jungle". If one of the matured heads gets too heavy and falls off, it becomes an Exeggcute.

Special Moves

Stomp, Egg Bomb, Wood Hammer

EVOLUTION

Exeggcute → Exeggutor

CUBONE

Pokémon Data

Lonely Pokémon

TYPE	Ground
	. . .
ABILITIES	Rock Head
	Lightningrod
HEIGHT	1´4″
WEIGHT	14.3 lb.

National Pokédex No.
104

Description

Sometimes Cubone cries, remembering its mother. When it does so the skull it wears on its head rattles. The marks on the skull are stains from its tears.

Special Moves

Bone Club, Headbutt, Focus Energy, Rage

1-49
50-99
100-149
150-199
200-249
250-299
300-349
350-399
400-449
450-491

EVO LUT ION

Cubone → Marowak

MAROWAK

Pokémon Data

Bone Keeper Pokémon

TYPE	Ground
	. . .
ABILITIES	Rock Head
	Lightningrod
HEIGHT	1′4″
WEIGHT	14.3 lb.

National Pokédex No.
105

Description

Marowak holds a bone from the moment it's born and can use it like a boomerang. It continues to use bones as weapons as it grows, and its personality becomes fiercer.

Special Moves

Bonemerang, Thrash, Bone Rush

EVO LUT ION

Cubone

Marowak

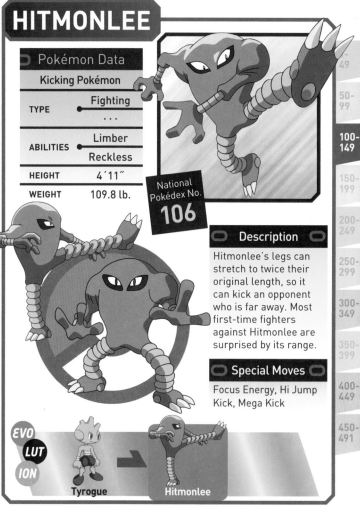

HITMONLEE

Pokémon Data

Kicking Pokémon

TYPE	Fighting
	...
ABILITIES	Limber
	Reckless
HEIGHT	4'11"
WEIGHT	109.8 lb.

National Pokédex No.
106

Description

Hitmonlee's legs can stretch to twice their original length, so it can kick an opponent who is far away. Most first-time fighters against Hitmonlee are surprised by its range.

Special Moves

Focus Energy, Hi Jump Kick, Mega Kick

EVO LUT ION

Tyrogue → Hitmonlee

49

50-
99

100-
149

150-
199

200-
249

250-
299

300-
349

350-
399

400-
449

450-
491

HITMONCHAN

Pokémon Data

Punching Pokémon

TYPE	Fighting
	. . .
ABILITIES	Keen Eye
	Iron Fist
HEIGHT	4′7″
WEIGHT	110.7 lb.

National Pokédex No.
107

Description

Hitmonchan's corkscrew punches are strong enough to destroy concrete. It might seem like it's standing still, but it's actually throwing punches too fast to be seen with the naked eye.

Special Moves

Vacuum Wave, Sky Uppercut, Counter

EVO
LUT
ION

Tyrogue   →   Hitmonchan

LICKITUNG

Pokémon Data

Licking Pokémon

TYPE	Normal . . .
ABILITIES	Own Tempo Oblivious
HEIGHT	3′11″
WEIGHT	144.4 lb.

National Pokédex No.
108

Description

Its tongue can extend twice as long as Lickitung is tall. The tongue is as dexterous as a hand and its slimy saliva can make anything stick to it.

Special Moves

Lick, Stomp, Wrap

EVO LUT ION

Lickitung   Lickilicky

1-49
50-99
100-149
150-199
200-249
250-299
300-349
350-399
400-449
450-491

KOFFING

Pokémon Data

Poison Gas Pokémon	
TYPE	Poison . . .
ABILITIES	Levitate . . .
HEIGHT	2′0″
WEIGHT	2.2 lb.

National Pokédex No.
109

Description

Koffing floats because its body is filled with a gas that's lighter than air. This gas is a combination of the vapors from fermenting trash and Koffing's own poisonous fumes.

Special Moves

SmokeScreen, Smog, Selfdestruct, Sludge

EVO LUT ION

Koffing → Weezing

WEEZING

Pokémon Data

Poison Gas Pokémon

TYPE	Poison
	...
ABILITIES	Levitate
	...
HEIGHT	3´11"
WEIGHT	20.9 lb.

National Pokédex No. **110**

Description

Weezing likes to feed on the gases emitted by decomposing trash. It infests dirty houses and raids the trash in the middle of the night.

Special Moves

Explosion, Sludge Bomb, Memento

1–49
50–99
100–149
150–199
200–249
250–299
300–349
350–399
400–449
450–491

EVO LUT ION

Koffing → Weezing

RHYHORN

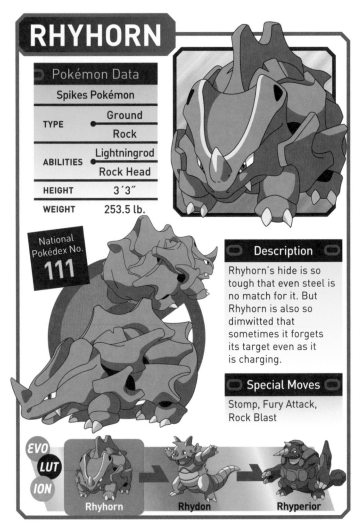

Pokémon Data

Spikes Pokémon

TYPE	Ground
	Rock
ABILITIES	Lightningrod
	Rock Head
HEIGHT	3'3"
WEIGHT	253.5 lb.

National Pokédex No.
111

Description

Rhyhorn's hide is so tough that even steel is no match for it. But Rhyhorn is also so dimwitted that sometimes it forgets its target even as it is charging.

Special Moves

Stomp, Fury Attack, Rock Blast

EVO LUT ION

Rhyhorn → Rhydon → Rhyperior

RHYDON

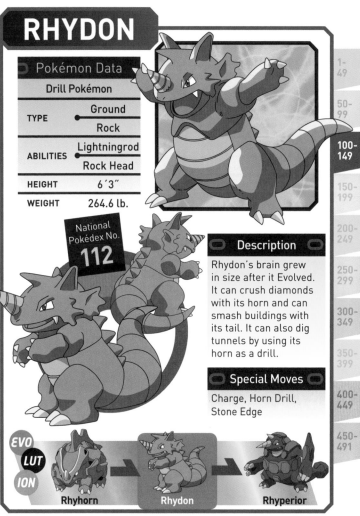

Pokémon Data

Drill Pokémon

TYPE	Ground
	Rock
ABILITIES	Lightningrod
	Rock Head
HEIGHT	6′3″
WEIGHT	264.6 lb.

National Pokédex No.
112

Description

Rhydon's brain grew in size after it Evolved. It can crush diamonds with its horn and can smash buildings with its tail. It can also dig tunnels by using its horn as a drill.

Special Moves

Charge, Horn Drill, Stone Edge

EVO LUT ION

Rhyhorn ➤ Rhydon ➤ Rhyperior

1-49
50-99
100-149
150-199
200-249
250-299
300-349
350-399
400-449
450-491

CHANSEY

Pokémon Data

Egg Pokémon

TYPE	Normal
	. . .
ABILITIES	Natural Cure
	Serene Grace
HEIGHT	3´7˝
WEIGHT	76.3 lb.

National Pokédex No.
113

Description

Chansey lays several eggs a day and will share them with those who are hurt, but it will never give one to a bad person. It is a Pokémon said to carry happiness with it.

Special Moves

Softboiled, Doubleslap, Egg Bomb, Double-Edge

EVO LUT ION

Happiny → Chansey → Blissey

TANGELA

Pokémon Data

Vine Pokémon

TYPE	Grass
	. . .
ABILITIES	Chlorophyll
	Leaf Guard
HEIGHT	3′3″
WEIGHT	77.2 lb.

National Pokédex No.
114

Description

Tangela's true form is unknown since it is covered in a mass of tangled blue vines. The vines undulate like seaweed as it walks.

Special Moves

Vine Whip, Bind, Mega Drain

EVO LUT ION

Tangela

Tangrowth

1-49
50-99
100-149
150-199
200-249
250-299
300-349
350-399
400-449
450-491

KANGASKHAN

Pokémon Data

Parent Pokémon	
TYPE	Normal
	...
ABILITIES	Early Bird
	Scrappy
HEIGHT	7′3″
WEIGHT	176.4 lb.

National Pokédex No.
115

Description

Kangaskhan raises its offspring in its belly pouch. After about three years, the young Kangaskhan strikes out on its own.

Special Moves

Mega Punch, Endure, Double Hit

EVOLUTION

Kangaskhan

Does not Evolve

HORSEA

Pokémon Data

Dragon Pokémon

TYPE	Water
	. . .
ABILITIES	Swift Swim
	Sniper
HEIGHT	1′4″
WEIGHT	17.6 lb.

1-49

50-99

100-149

150-199

200-249

250-299

300-349

350-399

400-449

450-491

Description

Horsea makes its nest among coral colonies, where it feeds on algae and tiny sea creatures. If the current gets too strong, it will anchor itself by wrapping its tail around the coral.

Special Moves

Water Gun, BubbleBeam, Focus Energy

National Pokédex No. **116**

EVO LUT ION

Horsea   Seadra   Kingdra

SEADRA

Pokémon Data

Dragon Pokémon	
TYPE	Water
	. . .
ABILITIES	Poison Point
	Sniper
HEIGHT	3´11˝
WEIGHT	55.1 lb.

Description

Seadra protects itself using its poisonous spikes. It weakens its prey by whirling its tail to create a whirlpool, and then it swallows its prey whole.

National Pokédex No.
117

Special Moves

Twister, Hydro Pump, Dragon Dance

EVO LUT ION

Horsea Seadra Kingdra

GOLDEEN

Pokémon Data

Goldfish Pokémon

TYPE	Water
	. . .
ABILITIES	Swift Swim
	Water Veil
HEIGHT	2´0˝
WEIGHT	33.1 lb.

National Pokédex No.
118

Description

Goldeen is known as the "Queen of the Water" because of its beauty. If it´s ever placed in an aquarium, it will use its horn to break the glass and escape.

Special Moves

Water Sport, Horn Attack, Water Pulse

EVO LUT ION

Goldeen → Seaking

1–49
50–99
100–149
150–199
200–249
250–299
300–349
350–399
400–449
450–491

SEAKING

Pokémon Data

Goldfish Pokémon

TYPE	Water
	. . .
ABILITIES	Swift Swim
	Water Veil
HEIGHT	4´3˝
WEIGHT	86.0 lb.

Description

Seaking creates a nest for its eggs by using its horn to dig into the river bottom. Until the eggs hatch, it keeps watch around the nest and will protect the eggs with its life.

National Pokédex No.
119

Special Moves

Waterfall, Agility, Megahorn

EVOLUTION

Goldeen → Seaking

STARYU

Pokémon Data

Star Shape Pokémon

TYPE	Water
	...
ABILITIES	Illuminate
	Natural Cure
HEIGHT	2'7"
WEIGHT	76.1 lb.

National Pokédex No.
120

Description

Staryu's central red core blinks off and on during the night; it seems to be communicating with the stars. As long as it retains its core, it can regenerate body parts that have been torn off.

Special Moves

Swift, Recover, Rapid Spin, BubbleBeam

EVO LUT ION

Staryu → Starmie

1-49
50-99
100-149
150-199
200-249
250-299
300-349
350-399
400-449
450-491

STARMIE

Pokémon Data

Mysterious Pokémon

TYPE	Water
	Psychic
ABILITIES	Illuminate
	Natural Cure
HEIGHT	3′7″
WEIGHT	176.4 lb.

National Pokédex No.
121

Description

The center of Starmie's body is composed of a gem-like, shimmering, rainbow-colored core. It transmits electronic signals from its core into the night sky.

Special Moves

Recover, Confuse Ray

EVO LUT ION

Staryu → Starmie

MR. MIME

Pokémon Data

Barrier Pokémon

TYPE	Psychic
	. . .
ABILITIES	Soundproof
	Filter
HEIGHT	4′3″
WEIGHT	120.1 lb.

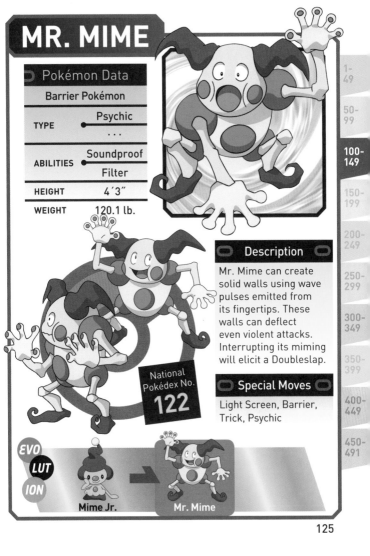

National Pokédex No.
122

Description

Mr. Mime can create solid walls using wave pulses emitted from its fingertips. These walls can deflect even violent attacks. Interrupting its miming will elicit a Doubleslap.

Special Moves

Light Screen, Barrier, Trick, Psychic

EVO LUT ION

Mime Jr. → Mr. Mime

1-49
50-99
100-149
150-199
200-249
250-299
300-349
350-399
400-449
450-491

SCYTHER

Pokémon Data

Mantis Pokémon

TYPE	Bug
	Flying
ABILITIES	Swarm
	Technician
HEIGHT	4′11″
WEIGHT	123.5 lb.

Description

It is extremely difficult to defend against an attack by Scyther if it uses both its arms. Its movements are so fast that it seems as if there are several Scythers at once.

National Pokédex No.

123

Special Moves

Wing Attack, Fury Cutter, Razor Wind

EVO LUT ION

Scyther → Scizor

JYNX

Pokémon Data

Human Shape Pokémon

TYPE	Ice
	Psychic
ABILITIES	Oblivious
	Forewarn
HEIGHT	4′7″
WEIGHT	89.5 lb.

National Pokédex No.
124

Description

Jynx's vocalizations are very similar to human speech, but the meaning behind them is unknown. Watching the rhythmic way Jynx walks might trigger a sudden urge to dance.

Special Moves

Avalanche, Blizzard, Lovely Kiss

EVO LUT ION

Smoochum

Jynx

49
50-99
100-149
150-199
200-249
250-299
300-349
350-399
400-449
450-491

ELECTABUZZ

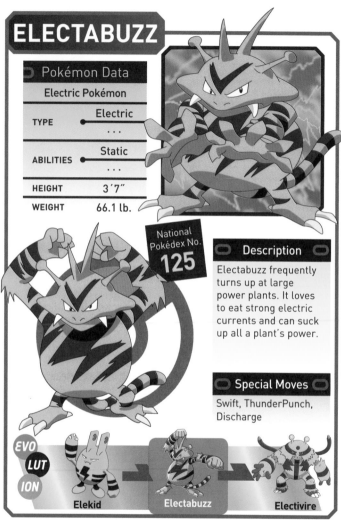

Pokémon Data

Electric Pokémon

TYPE	Electric
	...
ABILITIES	Static
	...
HEIGHT	3′7″
WEIGHT	66.1 lb.

National Pokédex No.
125

Description

Electabuzz frequently turns up at large power plants. It loves to eat strong electric currents and can suck up all a plant's power.

Special Moves

Swift, ThunderPunch, Discharge

EVO LUT ION

Elekid   Electabuzz   Electivire

MAGMAR

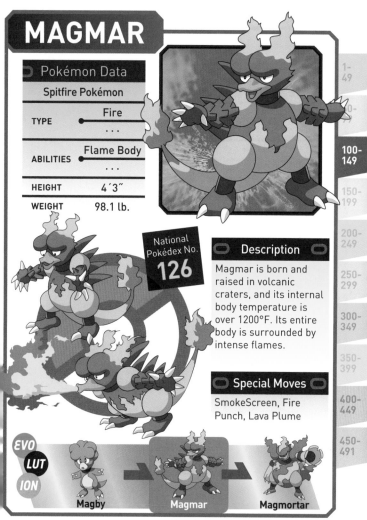

Pokémon Data

Spitfire Pokémon

TYPE	Fire
	...
ABILITIES	Flame Body
	...
HEIGHT	4′3″
WEIGHT	98.1 lb.

National Pokédex No. **126**

Description

Magmar is born and raised in volcanic craters, and its internal body temperature is over 1200°F. Its entire body is surrounded by intense flames.

Special Moves

SmokeScreen, Fire Punch, Lava Plume

EVO LUT ION

Magby → Magmar → Magmortar

1-49
100-149
150-199
200-249
250-299
300-349
350-399
400-449
450-491

PINSIR

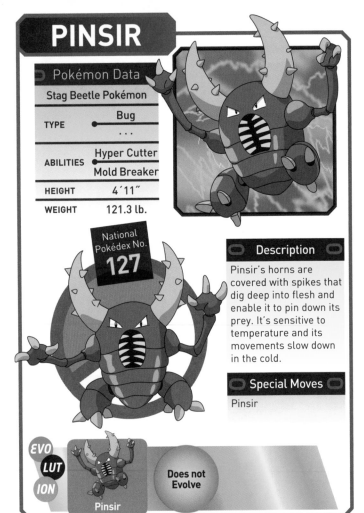

Pokémon Data

Stag Beetle Pokémon

TYPE	Bug
	...
ABILITIES	Hyper Cutter
	Mold Breaker
HEIGHT	4′11″
WEIGHT	121.3 lb.

National Pokédex No.
127

Description

Pinsir's horns are covered with spikes that dig deep into flesh and enable it to pin down its prey. It's sensitive to temperature and its movements slow down in the cold.

Special Moves

Pinsir

EVO LUT ION

Pinsir

Does not Evolve

TAUROS

Pokémon Data

Wild Bull Pokémon

TYPE	Normal
	. . .
ABILITIES	Intimidate
	Anger Point
HEIGHT	4'7"
WEIGHT	194.9 lb.

Description

Once Tauros zeroes in on its opponent, it charges forward in a straight line of attack, whipping itself on with its three tails. It has a tough and spirited personality.

Special Moves

Rage, Horn Attack, Tackle, Thrash

National Pokédex No.
128

EVO LUT ION

Tauros

Does not Evolve

1-49
50-99
100-149
150-199
200-249
250-299
300-349
350-399
400-449
450-491

MAGIKARP

Pokémon Data

Fish Pokémon

TYPE	Water
	. . .
ABILITIES	Swift Swim
	. . .
HEIGHT	2′11″
WEIGHT	22.0 lb.

National Pokédex No.
129

Description

For some reason, Magikarp is always leaping and splashing about. It's rumored to be the world's weakest Pokémon but was said to be more powerful eons ago.

Special Moves

Splash, Tackle, Flail

EVO LUT ION

Magikarp → Gyarados

GYARADOS

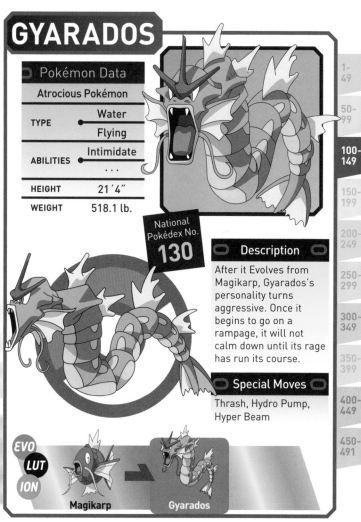

Pokémon Data

Atrocious Pokémon

TYPE	Water
	Flying
ABILITIES	Intimidate
	. . .
HEIGHT	21´4˝
WEIGHT	518.1 lb.

National Pokédex No.
130

Description

After it Evolves from Magikarp, Gyarados's personality turns aggressive. Once it begins to go on a rampage, it will not calm down until its rage has run its course.

Special Moves

Thrash, Hydro Pump, Hyper Beam

EVO LUT ION

Magikarp → Gyarados

1-49
50-99
100-149
150-199
200-249
250-299
300-349
350-399
400-449
450-491

LAPRAS

Pokémon Data

Transport Pokémon	
TYPE	Water
	Ice
ABILITIES	Water Absorb
	Shell Armor
HEIGHT	8′2″
WEIGHT	485.0 lb.

National Pokédex No.
131

Description

Lapras was overhunted in the past, so it is now rarely seen. It loves to travel the seas carrying humans or Pokémon on its back. It can understand human speech.

Special Moves

Water Pulse, Brine, Sheer Cold

EVO LUT ION

Lapras

Does not Evolve

DITTO

1–49
50–99
100–149
150–199
200–249
250–299
300–349
350–399
400–449
450–491

Pokémon Data

Transform Pokémon

TYPE	Normal	
	. . .	
ABILITIES	Limber	
	. . .	
HEIGHT	1′0″	
WEIGHT	8.8 lb.	

Description

Ditto has the power to instantaneously copy another being's cellular structure and transform itself into an exact replica. However, it has a hard time doing this from memory.

National Pokédex No.
132

Special Moves

Transform

EVO LUT ION

Ditto — Does not Evolve

135

EEVEE

Pokémon Data

Evolution Pokémon

TYPE	Normal
	...
ABILITIES	Run Away
	Adaptability
HEIGHT	1´0˝
WEIGHT	14.3 lb.

Description

A Pokémon with unstable genes, it adapts to extreme environments by transforming its appearance and powers. Evee is a highly unusual Pokémon.

National Pokédex No.
133

Special Moves

Growl, Quick Attack, Bite

EVOLUTION

Eevee → Jolteon, Vaporeon, Flareon, Espeon, Umbreon, Leafeon, Glaceon

VAPOREON

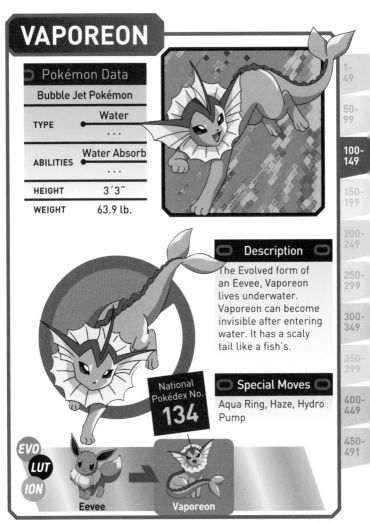

Pokémon Data

Bubble Jet Pokémon

TYPE	Water
	. . .
ABILITIES	Water Absorb
	. . .
HEIGHT	3′3″
WEIGHT	63.9 lb.

1–
49

50–
99

100–
149

150–
199

200–
249

250–
299

300–
349

350–
399

400–
449

450–
491

Description

The Evolved form of an Eevee, Vaporeon lives underwater. Vaporeon can become invisible after entering water. It has a scaly tail like a fish's.

National Pokédex No.
134

Special Moves

Aqua Ring, Haze, Hydro Pump

EVO LUT ION

Eevee ➡ Vaporeon

JOLTEON

Pokémon Data

Lightning Pokémon

TYPE	Electric . . .
ABILITIES	Volt Absorb . . .
HEIGHT	2′7″
WEIGHT	54.0 lb.

National Pokédex No.
135

Description

Jolteon can absorb the negative ions in the air and then blast bolts of electricity of up to 10,000 volts. Its fur stands on end when it is angry or startled.

Special Moves

Thunder Fang, Thunder Wave, Thunder

EVO LUT ION

Eevee → Jolteon

138

FLAREON

Pokémon Data

Flame Pokémon

TYPE	Fire
	. . .
ABILITIES	Flash Fire
	. . .
HEIGHT	2´11˝
WEIGHT	55.1 lb.

Description

Flareon has a fire chamber within its body. After taking a deep breath, it can blast out flames of 1700°F. Its internal temperature can rise to 900°F during battle.

Special Moves

Fire Fang, Smog, Fire Blast

National Pokédex No.
136

EVO LUT ION

Eevee → Flareon

1–
49
50–
99
100–
149
150–
199
200–
249
250–
299
300–
349
350–
399
400–
449
450–
491

PORYGON

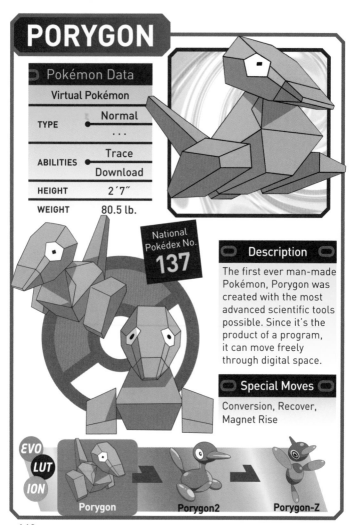

Pokémon Data

Virtual Pokémon

TYPE	Normal
	. . .
ABILITIES	Trace
	Download
HEIGHT	2′7″
WEIGHT	80.5 lb.

National Pokédex No.
137

Description

The first ever man-made Pokémon, Porygon was created with the most advanced scientific tools possible. Since it's the product of a program, it can move freely through digital space.

Special Moves

Conversion, Recover, Magnet Rise

EVO LUT ION

Porygon → Porygon2 → Porygon-Z

140

OMANYTE

1-49
50-99
100-149
150-199
200-249
250-299
300-349
350-399
400-449
450-491

Pokémon Data

Spiral Pokémon

TYPE	Rock
	Water
ABILITIES	Swift Swim
	Shell Armor
HEIGHT	1′4″
WEIGHT	16.5 lb.

National Pokédex No.

138

Description

An aquatic Pokémon that lived in prehistoric times, Omanyte was resurrected by scientists from a fossil of its helical shell. It swims by wriggling its ten legs.

Special Moves

Protect, AncientPower, Bite

EVO LUT ION

Omanyte   Omastar

OMASTAR

Pokémon Data

Spiral Pokémon	
TYPE	Rock
	Water
ABILITIES	Swift Swim
	Shell Armor
HEIGHT	3′3″
WEIGHT	77.2 lb.

National Pokédex No.
139

Description

Omastar was believed to have gone extinct because the shell on its back became too large, preventing it from being able to capture prey. It has a sharp beak and dextrous tentacles.

Special Moves

Tickle, Rock Blast, Hydro Pump

EVO LUT ION

Omanyte → Omastar

KABUTO

Pokémon Data

Shellfish Pokémon

TYPE	Rock
	Water
ABILITIES	Swift Swim
	Battle Armor
HEIGHT	1′8″
WEIGHT	25.4 lb.

1–49

50–99

100–149

150–199

200–249

250–299

300–349

350–399

400–449

450–491

National Pokédex No.

140

Description

Kabuto lived on sandy beaches 300 million years ago. It was resurrected from a fossil discovered in an area of land that had been the floor of an ancient ocean.

Special Moves

Harden, Absorb, Aqua Jet

EVO LUT ION

Kabuto → Kabutops

KABUTOPS

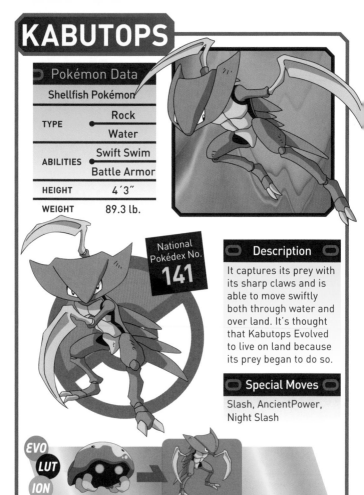

Pokémon Data

Shellfish Pokémon

TYPE	Rock
	Water
ABILITIES	Swift Swim
	Battle Armor
HEIGHT	4′3″
WEIGHT	89.3 lb.

National Pokédex No.
141

Description

It captures its prey with its sharp claws and is able to move swiftly both through water and over land. It's thought that Kabutops Evolved to live on land because its prey began to do so.

Special Moves

Slash, AncientPower, Night Slash

EVOLUTION

Kabuto → Kabutops

AERODACTYL

Pokémon Data

Fossil Pokémon

TYPE	Rock
	Flying
ABILITIES	Rock Head
	Pressure
HEIGHT	5´11˝
WEIGHT	130.1 lb.

National Pokédex No.

142

Description

Scientists re-created Aerodactyl from genetic material trapped in amber. It has teeth like saws and screeches loudly as it soars through the sky.

Special Moves

Wing Attack, Crunch, Rock Slide

1-

50-
99

100-
149

150-
199

200-
249

250-
299

300-
349

350-
399

400-
449

450-
491

EVO LUT ION

Aerodactyl

Does not Evolve

SNORLAX

Pokémon Data

Sleeping Pokémon

TYPE	Normal ...
ABILITIES	Immunity Thick Fat
HEIGHT	6'11"
WEIGHT	1014.1 lb.

National Pokédex No.
143

Description

Except for when it's sleeping, Snorlax is eating. It consumes over 800 pounds of food a day. Not surprisingly, it just keeps getting fatter.

Special Moves

Yawn, Rest, Sleep Talk, Giga Impact

EVO LUT ION

Munchlax → Snorlax

ARTICUNO

Pokémon Data

Freeze Pokémon

TYPE	Ice
	Flying
ABILITIES	Pressure
	. . .
HEIGHT	5′7″
WEIGHT	122.1 lb.

National Pokédex No.
144

Description

Articuno creates blizzards by freezing water particles in the air. One of the three Legendary Bird Pokémon of the Kanto region.

Special Moves

Blizzard, Sheer Cold, Ice Beam, Tailwind

EVO LUT ION

Articuno — Does not Evolve

1-49
50-99
100-149
150-199
200-249
250-299
300-349
350-399
400-449
450-491

ZAPDOS

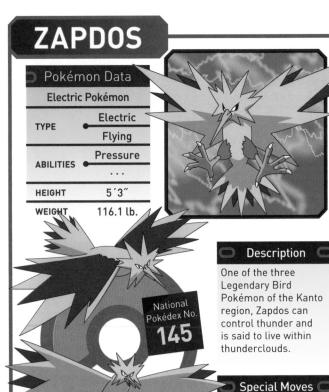

Pokémon Data

Electric Pokémon

TYPE	Electric
	Flying
ABILITIES	Pressure
	. . .
HEIGHT	5´3″
WEIGHT	116.1 lb.

National Pokédex No.
145

Description

One of the three Legendary Bird Pokémon of the Kanto region, Zapdos can control thunder and is said to live within thunderclouds.

Special Moves

Discharge, Drill Peck, Thunder

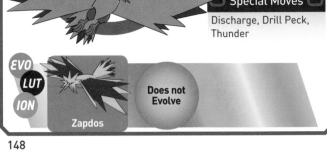

EVO LUT ION

Zapdos

Does not Evolve

MOLTRES

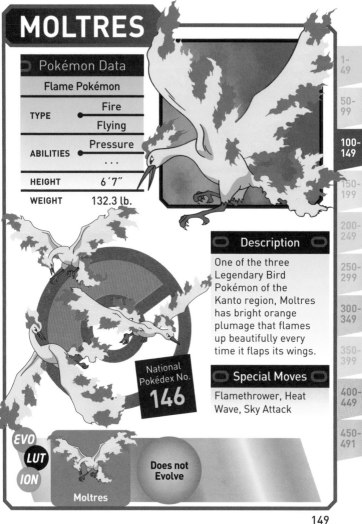

Pokémon Data

Flame Pokémon

TYPE	Fire
	Flying
ABILITIES	Pressure
	. . .
HEIGHT	6′7″
WEIGHT	132.3 lb.

1-
49

50-
99

**100-
149**

150-
199

200-
249

250-
299

300-
349

350-
399

400-
449

450-
491

Description

One of the three Legendary Bird Pokémon of the Kanto region, Moltres has bright orange plumage that flames up beautifully every time it flaps its wings.

National Pokédex No.
146

Special Moves

Flamethrower, Heat Wave, Sky Attack

EVO LUT ION

Moltres

Does not Evolve

149

DRATINI

Pokémon Data

Dragon Pokémon

TYPE	Dragon
	...
ABILITIES	Shed Skin
	...
HEIGHT	5´11˝
WEIGHT	7.3 lb.

National Pokédex No.
147

Description

Because it's so rare, for a long time it wasn't considered to be a real Pokémon. Dratini grows in stages, shedding its skin each time.

Special Moves

Wrap, Dragon Rage, Slam, Twister

EVO LUT ION

 Dratini → Dragonair → Dragonite

DRAGONAIR

Pokémon Data

Dragon Pokémon

TYPE	Dragon
	. . .
ABILITIES	Shed Skin
	. . .
HEIGHT	13′1″
WEIGHT	36.4 lb.

National Pokédex No.
148

Description

Dragonair lives in lakes and oceans. Weather changes can be predicted by the auras that surround its body. Although it does not have wings, it can fly.

Special Moves

Twister, Aqua Tail, Dragon Rush

EVO LUT ION

Dratini → Dragonair → Dragonite

1-49
50-99
100-149
150-199
200-249
250-299
300-349
350-399
400-449
450-491

DRAGONITE

Pokémon Data

Dragon Pokémon

TYPE	Dragon
	Flying
ABILITIES	Inner Focus
	. . .
HEIGHT	7′3″
WEIGHT	463.0 lb.

National Pokédex No.

149

Description

Dragonite live far out in the ocean and have been seen by very few humans. They will help the crews of shipwrecked boats by guiding them back to land.

Special Moves

Wing Attack, Outrage, Hyper Beam

EVO LUT ION

Dratini → Dragonair → Dragonite

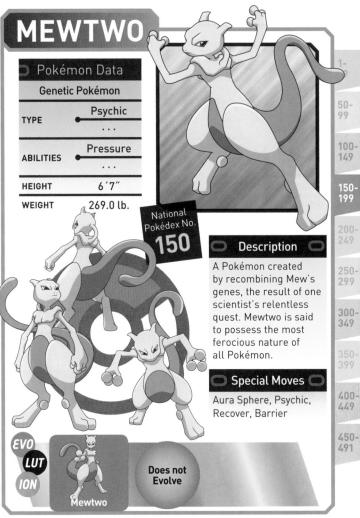

MEWTWO

Pokémon Data

Genetic Pokémon

TYPE	Psychic . . .
ABILITIES	Pressure . . .
HEIGHT	6′7″
WEIGHT	269.0 lb.

National Pokédex No.
150

Description

A Pokémon created by recombining Mew's genes, the result of one scientist's relentless quest. Mewtwo is said to possess the most ferocious nature of all Pokémon.

Special Moves

Aura Sphere, Psychic, Recover, Barrier

EVOLUTION

Mewtwo — Does not Evolve

1-
50-99
100-149
150-199
200-249
250-299
300-349
350-399
400-449
450-491

153

MEW

Pokémon Data

New Species Pokémon

TYPE	Psychic ...
ABILITIES	Synchronize ...
HEIGHT	1′4″
WEIGHT	8.8 lb.

Description

Mew can use an amazing number of attacks and can also appear and disappear at will. Mew is regarded by some scientists as the precursor to all modern-day Pokémon.

Special Moves

Psychic, Barrier, Amnesia

National Pokédex No.
151

EVO LUT ION

Mew

Does not Evolve

CHIKORITA

1-
49

50-
99

100-
149

150-
199

200-
249

250-
299

300-
349

350-
399

400-
449

450-
491

Pokémon Data

Leaf Pokémon

TYPE	Grass
	. . .
ABILITIES	Overgrow
	. . .
HEIGHT	2′11″
WEIGHT	14.1 lb.

National
Pokédex No.
152

Description

Chikorita is very mild-
mannered and loves
to bask in the sun. It
can read the humidity
and temperature of the
surrounding area using
the sweet-smelling
leaf on its head.

Special Moves

Razor Leaf, Synthesis,
PoisonPowder

EVO LUT ION

Chikorita

Bayleef

Meganium

BAYLEEF

Pokémon Data

Leaf Pokémon

TYPE	Grass
	...
ABILITIES	Overgrow
	...
HEIGHT	3´11″
WEIGHT	34.8 lb.

National Pokédex No.
153

Description

The buds around Bayleef's neck have a very sharp, distinctive scent that energizes those who smell it, so much so that they may even get aggressive.

Special Moves

Magical Leaf, Sweet Scent, Body Slam

EVO LUT ION

Chikorita

Bayleef

Meganium

MEGANIUM

Pokémon Data

Herb Pokémon

TYPE	Grass
	. . .
ABILITIES	Overgrow
	. . .
HEIGHT	5'11"
WEIGHT	221.6 lb.

National Pokédex No.

154

Description

Meganium's breath can bring dead grasses and flowers back to life. The scent from the petals around its neck has the power to calm an aggressive heart.

Special Moves

Petal Dance, Body Slam, Aromatherapy, Solarbeam

EVO LUT ION

 Chikorita

Bayleef

 Meganium

1-49

50-99

100-149

150-199

200-249

250-299

300-349

350-399

400-449

450-491

CYNDAQUIL

Pokémon Data

Fire Mouse Pokémon

TYPE	Fire
	. . .
ABILITIES	Blaze
	. . .
HEIGHT	1´8˝
WEIGHT	17.4 lb.

National Pokédex No.
155

Description

Cyndaquil is timid in nature, but when it's angered or surprised flames burst out of its back. It uses the flames as a defense mechanism.

Special Moves

SmokeScreen, Ember, Quick Attack

EVO LUT ION

Cyndaquil

Quilava

Typhlosion

QUILAVA

1–
49

50–
99

100–
149

150–
199

200–
249

250–
299

300–
349

350–
399

400–
449

450–
491

Pokémon Data

Volcano Pokémon

TYPE	Fire
	. . .

ABILITIES	Blaze
	. . .

HEIGHT	2´11˝
WEIGHT	41.9 lb.

National Pokédex No.
156

Description

Quilava uses the heat of its flames to intimidate opponents; the intensity of the flames increases in battle. The fur on its body is flame retardant.

Special Moves

Flame Wheel, Lava Plume, Flamethrower

EVO LUT ION

Cyndaquil → Quilava → Typhlosion

159

TYPHLOSION

Pokémon Data

Volcano Pokémon

TYPE	Fire
	. . .
ABILITIES	Blaze
	. . .
HEIGHT	5′7″
WEIGHT	175.3 lb.

National Pokédex No.
157

Description

Typhlosion ignites fire blasts by rubbing its hairs against one other. It uses the resulting heat haze to hide itself. Anything touching it while it is aroused will go up in flames instantly.

Special Moves

Flamethrower, Lava Plume, Eruption

EVOLUTION

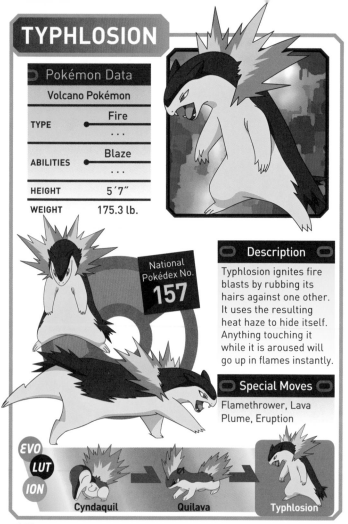

Cyndaquil · Quilava · Typhlosion

TOTODILE

1–
49

50–
99

100–
149

150–
199

200–
249

250–
299

300–
349

350–
399

400–
449

450–
491

Pokémon Data

Big Jaw Pokémon

TYPE	Water
	...
ABILITIES	Torrent
	...
HEIGHT	2'0"
WEIGHT	20.9 lb.

National
Pokédex No.
158

Description

Although it is small physically, Totodile can crush anything in its highly developed jaws. It instinctively bites anything that moves. Even its Trainer must be careful.

Special Moves

Water Gun, Bite, Thrash

EVO LUT ION

Totodile → Croconaw → Feraligatr

161

CROCONAW

Pokémon Data

Big Jaw Pokémon	
TYPE	Water
	. . .
ABILITIES	Torrent
	. . .
HEIGHT	3′7″
WEIGHT	55.1 lb.

National Pokédex No.
159

Description

Once Croconaw bites something and latches on with its big mouth, it does not let go until its teeth fall out. These teeth grow back quickly and it always has all forty-eight ready.

Special Moves

Rage, Crunch, Slash, Screech

EVO LUT ION

Totodile → Croconaw → Feraligatr

FERALIGATR

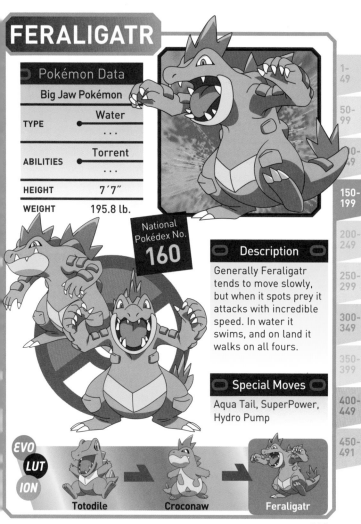

Pokémon Data

Big Jaw Pokémon	
TYPE	Water
	. . .
ABILITIES	Torrent
	. . .
HEIGHT	7′7″
WEIGHT	195.8 lb.

National Pokédex No.

160

Description

Generally Feraligatr tends to move slowly, but when it spots prey it attacks with incredible speed. In water it swims, and on land it walks on all fours.

Special Moves

Aqua Tail, SuperPower, Hydro Pump

EVOLUTION

Totodile → Croconaw → Feraligatr

1–49
50–99
100–149
150–199
200–249
250–299
300–349
350–399
400–449
450–491

SENTRET

Pokémon Data

Scout Pokémon

TYPE	Normal
	⋯
ABILITIES	Run Away
	Keen Eye
HEIGHT	2′7″
WEIGHT	13.2 lb.

National Pokédex No.
161

Description

Sentret is nervous by nature and always alert. It keeps watch far and wide by constantly stretching up on the tip of its tail. When it spots an enemy, it warns its companions.

Special Moves

Fury Swipes, Helping Hand, Slam

EVO LUT ION

Sentret → Furret

FURRET

Pokémon Data

Long Body Pokémon

TYPE	Normal
	. . .
ABILITIES	Run Away
	Keen Eye
HEIGHT	5′11″
WEIGHT	71.6 lb.

National
Pokédex No.
162

Description

A Furret nest is a complex maze, one suited to its long and flexible body. Although its limbs are short, it is very quick and nimble.

Special Moves

Rest, Me First, Hyper Voice

**EVO
LUT
ION**

Sentret

Furret

1-
49

50-
99

100-
149

150-
199

200-
249

250-
299

300-
349

350-
399

400-
449

450-
491

HOOTHOOT

Pokémon Data

Owl Pokémon

TYPE	Normal
	Flying
ABILITIES	Insomnia
	Keen Eye
HEIGHT	2'4"
WEIGHT	46.7 lb.

National Pokédex No.

163

Description

Hoothoot's internal rhythm is extremely accurate, and it calls out at the same time every day. It always stands on one foot; it changes feet so quickly no one can see it.

Special Moves

Hypnosis, Peck, Growl

EVO LUT ION

Hoothoot

Noctowl

NOCTOWL

Pokémon Data

Owl Pokémon

TYPE	Normal
	Flying
ABILITIES	Insomnia
	Keen Eye
HEIGHT	5'3"
WEIGHT	89.9 lb.

Description

If there's even the faintest amount of light, Noctowl can still see. When pondering difficult topics, it increases the effectiveness of its brain by turning its head upside down.

National Pokédex No.
164

Special Moves

Foresight, Air Slash, Zen Headbutt, Hypnosis

EVO
LUT
ION

Hoothoot   Noctowl

1–49

50–99

100–149

150–199

200–249

250–299

300–349

350–399

400–449

450–491

LEDYBA

Pokémon Data

Five Star Pokémon

TYPE	Bug
	Flying
ABILITIES	Swarm
	Early Bird
HEIGHT	3´3″
WEIGHT	23.8 lb.

National Pokédex No.

165

Description

Ledyba always group together; being alone makes them stricken with doubt and unable to move. When it gets cold, they huddle together for warmth.

Special Moves

Tackle, Supersonic, Comet Punch

EVO LUT ION

Ledyba

Ledian

LEDIAN

Pokémon Data

Five Star Pokémon

TYPE	Bug
	Flying
ABILITIES	Swarm
	Early Bird
HEIGHT	4′7″
WEIGHT	78.5 lb.

National Pokédex No.
166

Description

Ledian uses starlight as energy. On star-lit nights, it flies about scattering shimmering powder. The patterns on its back change depending on the stars in the night sky.

Special Moves

Tackle, Mach Punch, Bug Buzz

EVO LUT ION

Ledyba

Ledian

1–49

50–99

100–149

150–199

200–249

250–299

300–349

350–399

400–449

450–491

SPINARAK

Pokémon Data

String Spit Pokémon	
TYPE	Bug
	Poison
ABILITIES	Swarm
	Insomnia
HEIGHT	1´8˝
WEIGHT	18.7 lb.

National Pokédex No.
167

Description

Spinarak creates traps by spinning webs of fine but sturdy silk. It waits, motionless within its nest, until prey becomes entangled in its web.

Special Moves

String Shot, Leech Life, Night Shade

EVO LUT ION

Spinarak → Ariados

ARIADOS

Pokémon Data

Long Leg Pokémon	
TYPE	Bug
	Poison
ABILITIES	Swarm
	Insomnia
HEIGHT	3'7"
WEIGHT	73.9 lb.

National Pokédex No.
168

Description

Initially, Ariados allows its prey to escape, but it leaves a silk thread attached so it can follow later and capture its prey's companions as well.

Special Moves

Spider Web, Pin Missile, Poison Jab

EVO LUT ION

Spinarak → Ariados

1-49
50-99
100-149
150-199
200-249
250-299
300-349
350-399
400-449
450-491

CROBAT

Pokémon Data

Bat Pokémon

TYPE	Poison
	Flying
ABILITIES	Inner Focus
	. . .
HEIGHT	5'11"
WEIGHT	165.3 lb.

Description

Using its four wings, Crobat is able to fly faster and more quietly than it could before it Evolved. It rests by hanging upside-down from branches using its back wings.

National Pokédex No.
169

Special Moves

Cross Poison, Astonish, Haze

EVO LUT ION

Zubat → Golbat → Crobat

CHINCHOU

Pokémon Data

Angler Pokémon	
TYPE	Water
	Electric
ABILITIES	Volt Absorb
	Illuminate
HEIGHT	1´8˝
WEIGHT	26.5 lb.

National Pokédex No.
170

Description

Chinchou can run an extremely powerful electric current between its antennae. It shocks its prey by sending positive and negative bolts through the tips of its antennae.

Special Moves

Thunder Wave, Spark, Water Gun

EVO LUT ION

Chinchou   Lanturn

1-49
50-99
100-149
150-199
200-249
250-299
300-349
350-399
400-449
450-491

LANTURN

Pokémon Data

Light Pokémon	
TYPE	Water
	Electric
ABILITIES	Volt Absorb
	Illuminate
HEIGHT	3′11″
WEIGHT	49.6 lb.

National Pokédex No.
171

Description

Lanturn blinds its prey by shining a very bright light in their eyes, then swallows them whole while they are stunned. Because of the strength of its light, it's called the "Deep-Sea Star."

Special Moves

BubbleBeam, Discharge, Hydro Pump

EVO LUT ION

Chinchou → Lanturn

PICHU

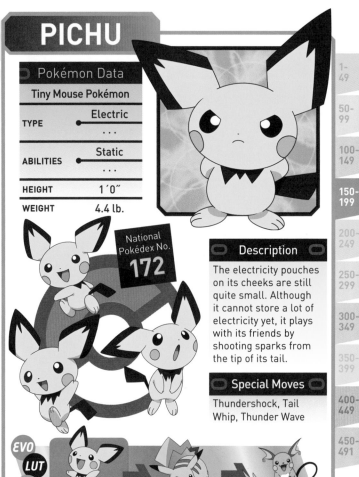

Pokémon Data

Tiny Mouse Pokémon

TYPE	Electric
	...
ABILITIES	Static
	...
HEIGHT	1´0″
WEIGHT	4.4 lb.

National Pokédex No.
172

Description

The electricity pouches on its cheeks are still quite small. Although it cannot store a lot of electricity yet, it plays with its friends by shooting sparks from the tip of its tail.

Special Moves

Thundershock, Tail Whip, Thunder Wave

EVO LUT ION

Pichu → Pikachu → Raichu

1-49
50-99
100-149
150-199
200-249
250-299
300-349
350-399
400-449
450-491

CLEFFA

Pokémon Data

Star Shape Pokémon

TYPE	Normal
	. . .
ABILITIES	Cute Charm
	Magic Guard
HEIGHT	1′0″
WEIGHT	6.6 lb.

National Pokédex No.
173

Description

Cleffa are shaped like stars and gather on nights when there are lots of shooting stars. Because of this, it's said that they came to Earth on shooting stars.

Special Moves

Charm, Sweet Kiss, Encore

EVO LUT ION

Cleffa

Clefairy

Clefable

IGGLYBUFF

Pokémon Data

Balloon Pokémon

TYPE	Normal
	. . .
ABILITIES	Cute Charm
	. . .
HEIGHT	1′0″
WEIGHT	2.2 lb.

National Pokédex No.
174

Description

Igglybuff's elastic body feels very nice to the touch. Once it starts bouncing it's quite hard to stop it. It can damage its throat if it keeps singing for a long time.

Special Moves

Defense Curl, Sing, Sweet Kiss

1-49
50-99
100-149
150-199
200-249
250-299
300-349
350-399
400-449
450-491

EVO LUT ION

Igglybuff   Jigglypuff   Wigglytuff

TOGEPI

Pokémon Data

Spike Ball Pokémon

TYPE	Normal
	. . .
ABILITIES	Hustle
	Serene Grace
HEIGHT	1′0″
WEIGHT	3.3 lb.

National Pokédex No.
175

Description

Togepi's shell is said to be stuffed to the brim with happiness, which it shares with kind-hearted people. Getting a sleeping Togepi to stand up also brings one happiness.

Special Moves

Metronome, Sweet Kiss, Yawn

EVO LUT ION

Togepi → Togetic → Togekiss

TOGETIC

Pokémon Data

Happiness Pokémon

TYPE	Normal
	Flying
ABILITIES	Hustle
	Serene Grace
HEIGHT	2´0″
WEIGHT	7.1 lb.

1-
49

50-
99

100-
149

150-
199

200-
249

250-
299

300-
349

350-
399

400-
449

450-
491

National
Pokédex No.
176

Description

Togetic appears before kind-hearted people and sprinkles them with a glowing down known as "Joy Dust." It loses energy if it does not stay close to kind people.

Special Moves

Wish, Follow Me, Last Resort

EVO LUT ION

Togepi ➤ **Togetic** ➤ **Togekiss**

NATU

Pokémon Data

Tiny Bird Pokémon

TYPE	Psychic
	Flying
ABILITIES	Synchronize
	Early Bird
HEIGHT	0´8˝
WEIGHT	4.4 lb.

National Pokédex No.

177

Description

Since its wings have not fully grown yet, Natu cannot fly. Instead, it uses its jumping skills to move around. It eats cacti, skillfully picking its way around the buds and spines.

Special Moves

Teleport, Lucky Chant, Confuse Ray

EVOLUTION

Natu → Xatu

XATU

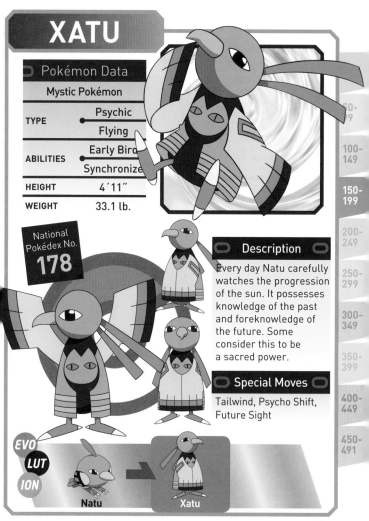

Pokémon Data

Mystic Pokémon

TYPE	Psychic
	Flying
ABILITIES	Early Bird
	Synchronize
HEIGHT	4′11″
WEIGHT	33.1 lb.

National Pokédex No.
178

Description

Every day Natu carefully watches the progression of the sun. It possesses knowledge of the past and foreknowledge of the future. Some consider this to be a sacred power.

Special Moves

Tailwind, Psycho Shift, Future Sight

EVOLUTION

Natu → Xatu

50-99
100-149
150-199
200-249
250-299
300-349
350-399
400-449
450-491

MAREEP

Pokémon Data

Wool Pokémon

TYPE	Electric . . .
ABILITIES	Static . . .
HEIGHT	2´0″
WEIGHT	17.2 lb

National Pokédex No.
179

Description

Static electricity is created when Mareep's wool is rubbed, and when this electricity builds up, its wool doubles in size. Anyone who touches it then will get an electric shock.

Special Moves

Growl, Thundershock, Thunder Wave

EVO LUT ION

Mareep → Flaaffy → Ampharos

FLAAFFY

Pokémon Data

Wool Pokémon

TYPE	Electric
	...
ABILITIES	Static
	...
HEIGHT	2′7″
WEIGHT	29.3 lb.

National Pokédex No.
180

Description

Electricity tends to build up in its wool, and when it's fully charged the ball on the tip of its tail glows. Because of its rubbery skin, Flaaffy itself is protected from electric shocks.

Special Moves

Cotton Spore, Charge, Discharge, Thunder

1-
49

50-
99

100-
149

150-
199

200-
249

250-
299

300-
349

350-
399

400-
449

450-
491

EVO LUT ION

Mareep → Flaaffy → Ampharos

AMPHAROS

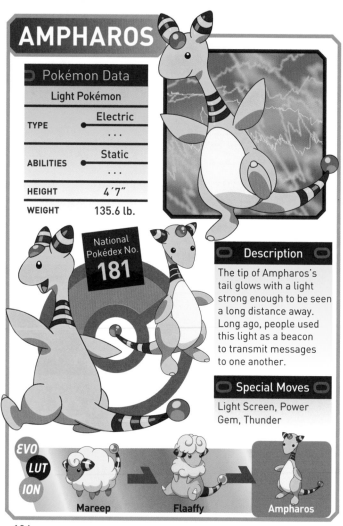

Pokémon Data

Light Pokémon

TYPE	Electric
	...
ABILITIES	Static
	...
HEIGHT	4'7"
WEIGHT	135.6 lb.

National Pokédex No.
181

Description

The tip of Ampharos's tail glows with a light strong enough to be seen a long distance away. Long ago, people used this light as a beacon to transmit messages to one another.

Special Moves

Light Screen, Power Gem, Thunder

EVO LUT ION

Mareep → Flaaffy → Ampharos

BELLOSSOM

1–
49

50–
99

100–
149

150–
199

200–
249

250–
299

300–
349

350–
399

400–
449

450–
491

Pokémon Data

Flower Pokémon

TYPE	Grass
	. . .
ABILITIES	Chlorophyll
	. . .
HEIGHT	1´4˝
WEIGHT	12.8 lb.

National Pokédex No.
182

Description

When the rainy season ends, Bellossom dances while basking in the warm rays of the sun. The stinkier it was as Gloom, the more beautiful as it will be as Bellossum.

Special Moves

Sweet Scent, Sunny Day, Leaf Storm

EVO
LUT
ION

Oddish   Gloom   Bellossom

185

MARILL

Pokémon Data

Aqua Mouse Pokémon

TYPE	Water
	. . .
ABILITIES	Thick Fat
	Huge Power
HEIGHT	1′4″
WEIGHT	18.7 lb.

Description

The ball at the tip of its tail is filled with an oil lighter than water. It uses the ball as a float when it dives down to feed on its favorite water grasses on riverbeds.

Special Moves

BubbleBeam, Water Gun, Defense Curl, Rollout

National Pokédex No.
183

EVO LUT ION

Azurill → Marill → Azumarill

186

AZUMARILL

Pokémon Data

Aqua Rabbit Pokémon

TYPE	Water
	. . .
ABILITIES	Thick Fat
	Huge Power
HEIGHT	2′7″
WEIGHT	62.8 lb.

National Pokédex No.
184

Description

Azumarill lives in rivers and lakes. It uses its long ears to pick up the sounds of its prey. When i´s in the water, it rolls up its ears so water doesn't get in them.

Special Moves

Aqua Ring, Rain Dance, Hydro Pump

EVOLUTION

Azurill ➤ Marill ➤ **Azumarill**

1-49
50-99
100-149
50-199
200-249
250-299
300-349
350-399
400-449
450-491

SUDOWOODO

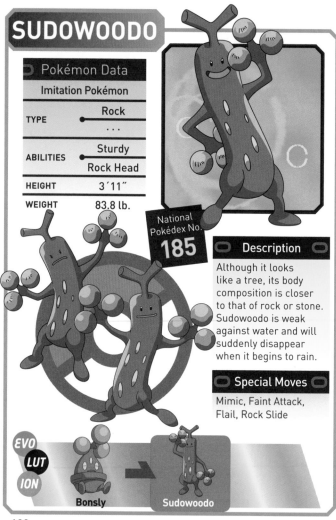

Pokémon Data

Imitation Pokémon

TYPE	Rock
	...
ABILITIES	Sturdy
	Rock Head
HEIGHT	3′11″
WEIGHT	83.8 lb.

National
Pokédex No.
185

Description

Although it looks like a tree, its body composition is closer to that of rock or stone. Sudowoodo is weak against water and will suddenly disappear when it begins to rain.

Special Moves

Mimic, Faint Attack, Flail, Rock Slide

EVO LUT ION

Bonsly → Sudowoodo

POLITOED

Pokémon Data

Frog Pokémon

TYPE	Water . . .
ABILITIES	Water Absorb Damp
HEIGHT	3′7″
WEIGHT	74.7 lb.

Description

Politoed calls together Poliwag and Poliwhirl to form a group with itself as the leader. When more than three Politoed assemble, they begin to sing in a chorus.

Special Moves

Bounce, Swagger, BubbleBeam

National Pokédex No.
186

EVO LUT ION

Poliwag ▶ Poliwhirl ▶ Politoed

1-49
50-99
100-149
150-199
200-249
250-299
300-349
350-399
400-449
450-491

HOPPIP

Pokémon Data

Cottonweed Pokémon

TYPE	Grass
	Flying
ABILITIES	Chlorophyll
	Leaf Guard
HEIGHT	1'4"
WEIGHT	1.1 lb.

National Pokédex No.

187

Description

Because Hoppip is so light, it frequently gets carried off by a breeze. It is said that when Hoppip congregate on the hills and fields, spring is just around the corner.

Special Moves

Splash, Tackle, Stun Spore, Poisonpowder

EVOLUTION

Hoppip ➤ Skiploom ➤ Jumpluff

SKIPLOOM

Pokémon Data

Cottonweed Pokémon

TYPE	Grass
	Flying
ABILITIES	Chlorophyll
	Leaf Guard
HEIGHT	2'0"
WEIGHT	2.2 lb.

National Pokédex No.

188

1-49

50-99

100-149

150-199

200-249

250-299

300-349

350-399

400-449

450-491

Description

The flower on the top of Skiploom's head blooms when the temperature rises and closes as it goes down. It floats about in the sky so that it can absorb the sun's rays.

Special Moves

Sleep Powder, Bullet Seed, Mega Drain

EVO LUT ION

Hoppip → Skiploom → Jumpluff

191

JUMPLUFF

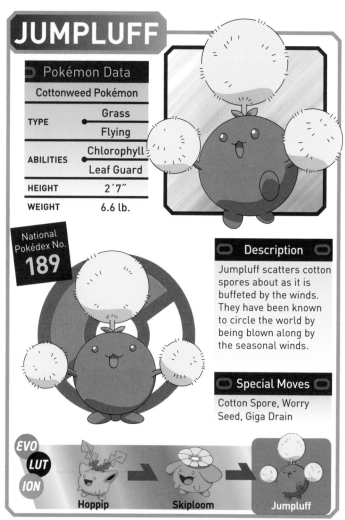

Pokémon Data

Cottonweed Pokémon

TYPE	Grass
	Flying
ABILITIES	Chlorophyll
	Leaf Guard
HEIGHT	2´7˝
WEIGHT	6.6 lb.

National Pokédex No.
189

Description

Jumpluff scatters cotton spores about as it is buffeted by the winds. They have been known to circle the world by being blown along by the seasonal winds.

Special Moves

Cotton Spore, Worry Seed, Giga Drain

EVO LUT ION

Hoppip → Skiploom → Jumpluff

AIPOM

Pokémon Data

Long Tail Pokémon

TYPE	Normal
	. . .
ABILITIES	Run Away
	Pickup
HEIGHT	2′7″
WEIGHT	25.4 lb

National Pokédex No.
190

Description

Aipom has a tail that is actually more dextrous than its hands, which is very useful when it needs to hang upside-down or when it needs to get food.

Special Moves

Tail Whip, Fury Swipes, Tickle

EVO LUT ION

Aipom → Ambipom

1-49
50-99
100-149
150-199
200-249
250-299
300-349
350-399
400-449
450-491

SUNKERN

Pokémon Data

Seed Pokémon

TYPE	Grass
	...
ABILITIES	Chlorophyll
	Solar Power
HEIGHT	1′0″
WEIGHT	4.0 lb.

Description

Sunkern survives on the morning dew that forms on its leaves. A cold summer generally points to a bumper crop the following year.

Special Moves

Ingrain, Leech Seed, Razor Leaf

National Pokédex No.
191

EVO LUT ION

Sunkern   Sunflora

SUNFLORA

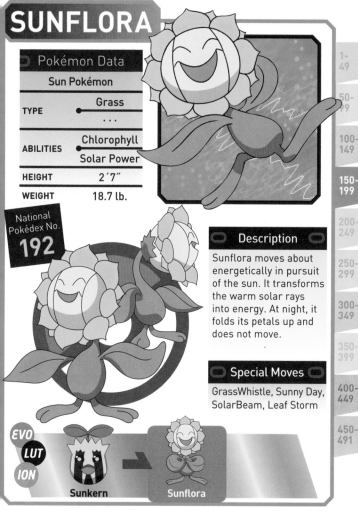

Pokémon Data

Sun Pokémon

TYPE	Grass
	. . .
ABILITIES	Chlorophyll
	Solar Power
HEIGHT	2′7″
WEIGHT	18.7 lb.

National Pokédex No.
192

Description

Sunflora moves about energetically in pursuit of the sun. It transforms the warm solar rays into energy. At night, it folds its petals up and does not move.

Special Moves

GrassWhistle, Sunny Day, SolarBeam, Leaf Storm

EVO LUT ION

Sunkern ⟶ Sunflora

1-49
50-99
100-149
150-199
200-249
250-299
300-349
350-399
400-449
450-491

195

YANMA

Pokémon Data

Clear Wing Pokémon

TYPE	Bug
	Flying
ABILITIES	Speed Boost
	Compoundeyes
HEIGHT	3′11″
WEIGHT	83.8 lb.

National Pokédex No.

193

Description

Thanks to its big eyes and 360° vision, Yanma can see everything in its vicinity and even catch prey that's behind it. The beating of its wings can cause shock waves.

Special Moves

Sonicboom, Detect, Supersonic, U-turn

EVO LUT ION

Yanma   Yanmega

WOOPER

1-
49

50-
99

100-
149

150-
199

200-
249

250-
299

300-
349

350-
399

400-
449

450-
491

Pokémon Data

Water Fish Pokémon

TYPE	Water
	Ground
ABILITIES	Damp
	Water Absorb
HEIGHT	1' 4"
WEIGHT	18.7 lb.

National Pokédex No.

194

Description

Wooper lives in cold waters. When it walks on land, it covers its body with a poisonous protective film. When it sleeps, it half-buries its body in mud.

Special Moves

Water Gun, Mud Sport, Mud Shot

EVO
LUT
ION

Wooper   Quagsire

QUAGSIRE

Pokémon Data

Water Fish Pokémon

TYPE	Water
	Ground
ABILITIES	Damp
	Water Absorb
HEIGHT	4'7"
WEIGHT	165.3 lb.

National Pokédex No.
195

Description

Quagsire lounges on river bottoms, waiting for prey. It's so easy-going that even if it bumps its head against rocks or boat bottoms while swimming, it doesn't mind.

Special Moves

Amnesia, Muddy Water, Earthquake, Yawn

EVOLUTION

Wooper → Quagsire

ESPEON

Pokémon Data

Sun Pokémon

TYPE	Psychic
	. . .
ABILITIES	Synchronize
	. . .
HEIGHT	2′11″
WEIGHT	58.4 lb.

National
Pokédex No.
196

Description

Espeon's body is covered in very fine fur. As air currents pass through its fur, it's able to sense things like changes in the weather or an opponent's next move.

Special Moves

Future Sight, Psych Up, Morning Sun

EVO LUT ION

Eevee → Espeon

1-49
50-99
100-149
150-199
200-249
250-299
300-349
350-399
400-449
450-491

UMBREON

Pokémon Data

Moonlight Pokémon

TYPE	Dark
	...
ABILITIES	Synchronize
	...
HEIGHT	3′3″
WEIGHT	59.5 lb.

National Pokédex No.
197

Description

An Umbreon is an Eevee transformed by the light of the moon. The ring patterns on its body glow when night falls. It secretes a poisonous sweat when it needs to defend itself.

Special Moves

Faint Attack, Assurance, Moonlight

EVO
LUT
ION

Eevee → Umbreon

200

MURKROW

Pokémon Data

Darkness Pokémon	
TYPE	Dark
	Flying
ABILITIES	Insomnia
	Super Luck
HEIGHT	1´8˝
WEIGHT	4.6 lb.

National Pokédex No.
198

Description

It's said that seeing a Murkrow at night will bring bad luck. They lure travelers onto mountain roads leading deep into the woods and get them utterly lost.

Special Moves

Astonish, Pursuit, Wing Attack, Sucker Punch

EVO LUT ION

Murkrow → Honchkrow

1-49
50-99
100-149
150-199
200-249
250-299
300-349
350-399
400-449
450-491

SLOWKING

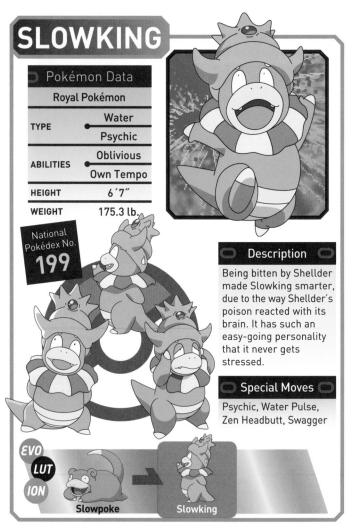

Pokémon Data

Royal Pokémon	
TYPE	Water
	Psychic
ABILITIES	Oblivious
	Own Tempo
HEIGHT	6'7"
WEIGHT	175.3 lb.

National Pokédex No.
199

Description

Being bitten by Shellder made Slowking smarter, due to the way Shellder's poison reacted with its brain. It has such an easy-going personality that it never gets stressed.

Special Moves

Psychic, Water Pulse, Zen Headbutt, Swagger

EVOLUTION

Slowpoke → Slowking

MISDREAVUS

Pokémon Data

Screech Pokémon	
TYPE	Ghost . . .
ABILITIES	Levitate . . .
HEIGHT	2'4"
WEIGHT	2.2 lb.

National Pokédex No.

200

Description

At night, Misdreavus entertains itself by sneaking up behind people and shrieking. It feeds off fear, which it absorbs and stores in the red orbs around its neck.

Special Moves

Astonish, Growl, Shadow Ball, Perish Song

EVO LUT ION

Misdreavus → Mismagius

1–49
50–99
100–149
150–199
200–249
250–299
300–349
350–399
400–449
450–491

UNOWN

Pokémon Data

Symbol Pokémon

TYPE	Psychic ...
ABILITIES	Levitate ...
HEIGHT	1´8˝
WEIGHT	11.0 lb.

National Pokédex No.

201

Description

Unown are usually found stuck to walls. They look like ancient glyphs, and their forms are said to have some hidden meaning. They are able to communicate telepathically.

Special Moves

Hidden Power

EVO LUT ION

Unown

Does not Evolve

WOBBUFFET

Pokémon Data

Patient Pokémon	
TYPE	Psychic · · ·
ABILITIES	Shadow Tag · · ·
HEIGHT	4´3″
WEIGHT	62.8 lb.

National Pokédex No.
202

1-49
50-99
100-149
150-199
200-249
250-299
300-349
350-399
400-449
450-491

Description

A stoic Pokémon that stays calm through practically anything—except when its tail is attacked. When two or more Wobbuffet gather, they play by testing each other's endurance.

Special Moves

Counter, Mirror Coat, Safeguard

EVO LUT ION

Wynaut   Wobbuffet

GIRAFARIG

Pokémon Data

Long Neck Pokémon

TYPE	Normal
	Psychic
ABILITIES	Inner Focus
	Early Bird
HEIGHT	4'11"
WEIGHT	91.5 lb.

National Pokédex No.
203

Description

The head of Girafarig's tail is able to attack by reacting to smells and sounds. Since the tail head does not need any sleep, it is constantly on the lookout.

Special Moves

Stomp, Double Hit, Psychic

EVO LUT ION

Girafarig

Does not Evolve

PINECO

Pokémon Data

Bagworm Pokémon	
TYPE	Bug
	...
ABILITIES	Sturdy
	...
HEIGHT	2′0″
WEIGHT	15.9 lb.

National Pokédex No.
204

Description

Pineco makes its shell thicker by layering it with tree bark. As it dangles from trees, waiting for prey, it's occasionally pecked at by birds who mistake it for a pinecone.

Special Moves

Selfdestruct, Rapid Spin, Natural Gift

EVOLUTION

Pineco → Forretress

1-49
50-99
100-149
150-199
200-249
250-299
300-349
350-399
400-449
450-491

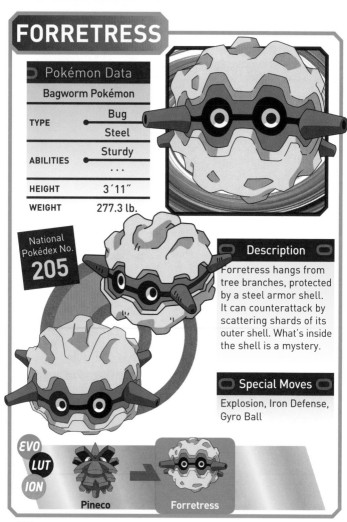

FORRETRESS

Pokémon Data

Bagworm Pokémon

TYPE	Bug
	Steel
ABILITIES	Sturdy
	. . .
HEIGHT	3´11″
WEIGHT	277.3 lb.

National Pokédex No.
205

Description

Forretress hangs from tree branches, protected by a steel armor shell. It can counterattack by scattering shards of its outer shell. What's inside the shell is a mystery.

Special Moves

Explosion, Iron Defense, Gyro Ball

EVO LUT ION

Pineco → Forretress

DUNSPARCE

Pokémon Data

Land Snake Pokémon

TYPE	Normal
	. . .
ABILITIES	Serene Grace
	Run Away
HEIGHT	4´11˝
WEIGHT	30.9 lb.

National Pokédex No.
206

-49
50-99
100-149
150-199
200-249
250-299
300-349
350-399
400-449
450-491

Description

Dunsparce digs a long, maze-like nest with its tail. If detected, it will escape by burrowing backwards. It can fly just a little.

Special Moves

Glare, Pursuit, Dig, Flail

EVO LUT ION

Dunsparce

Does not Evolve

GLIGAR

Pokémon Data

FlyScorpion Pokémon

TYPE	Ground
	Flying
ABILITIES	Hyper Cutter
	Sand Veil
HEIGHT	3′7″
WEIGHT	142.9 lb.

National Pokédex No.
207

Description

Gligar is usually found hanging on to the sides of cliffs; when its prey approaches, it swoops down and attacks. It latches onto the face of its prey and jabs with its poison stinger.

Special Moves

Poison Sting, Fury Cutter, Faint Attack

EVO LUT ION

Gligar → Gliscor

STEELIX

Pokémon Data

Iron Snake Pokémon

TYPE	Steel
	Ground

ABILITIES	Rock Head
	Sturdy
HEIGHT	30′2″
WEIGHT	881.8 lb.

National Pokédex No.
208

Description

Tempered by the earth's subterranean pressure and heat, Steelix's body is harder than diamonds or any metals. It moves through the earth, crushing rock as it goes along.

Special Moves

Crunch, Rock Polish, Iron Tail, Stone Edge

EVO LUT ION

Onix → Steelix

1- 49
50- 99
100- 149
150- 199
200- 249
250- 299
300- 349
350- 399
400- 449
450- 491

SNUBBULL

Pokémon Data

Fairy Pokémon	
TYPE	Normal
	...
ABILITIES	Intimidate
	Run Away
HEIGHT	2′0″
WEIGHT	17.2 lb.

National Pokédex No.
209

Description

Snubbull's face is so scary that small Pokémon run away in fright, but it is actually a very kind-hearted Pokémon. Very popular with women because it's devoted and loyal.

Special Moves

Tackle, Scary Face, Bite, Roar

EVOLUTION

Snubbull   Granbull

GRANBULL

Pokémon Data

Fairy Pokémon	
TYPE	Normal
	. . .
ABILITIES	Intimidate
	Run Away
HEIGHT	4′7″
WEIGHT	107.4 lb.

Description

Despite Granbull's fierce appearance, it is actually quite timid. But once it is angered, it will attack with its huge fangs.

Special Moves

Roar, Rage, Take Down, Crunch

National Pokédex No.
210

1-49
50-99
100-149
150-199
200-249
250-299
300-349
350-399
400-449
450-491

EVOLUTION

Snubbull — Granbull

QWILFISH

Pokémon Data

Balloon Pokémon

TYPE	Water
	Poison
ABILITIES	Poison Point
	Swift Swim
HEIGHT	1´8″
WEIGHT	8.6 lb.

National Pokédex No.
211

Description

It can shoot out the poisoned spines on its body in any direction, but in order to do so it must suck in water to puff up its body. But this makes it hard for Quilfish to swim.

Special Moves

Water Gun, Pin Missile, Poison Jab

EVOLUTION

Qwilfish

Does not Evolve

214

SCIZOR

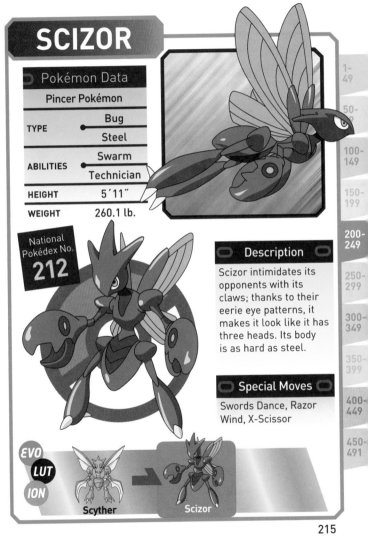

Pokémon Data

Pincer Pokémon

TYPE	Bug
	Steel
ABILITIES	Swarm
	Technician
HEIGHT	5′11″
WEIGHT	260.1 lb.

National Pokédex No.
212

Description

Scizor intimidates its opponents with its claws; thanks to their eerie eye patterns, it makes it look like it has three heads. Its body is as hard as steel.

Special Moves

Swords Dance, Razor Wind, X-Scissor

EVO LUT ION

Scyther → Scizor

1–49
50–
100–149
150–199
200–249
250–299
300–349
350–399
400–449
450–491

SHUCKLE

Pokémon Data

Mold Pokémon	
TYPE	Bug
	Rock
ABILITIES	Sturdy
	Gluttony
HEIGHT	2'0"
WEIGHT	45.2 lb.

National Pokédex No.

213

Description

Shuckle hides under rocks to avoid its enemies. It collects Berries and stores them in its shell, where they ferment into a delicious liquid.

Special Moves

Bide, Safeguard, Wrap, Gastro Acid

Shuckle

Does not Evolve

HERACROSS

Pokémon Data

Single Horn Pokémon

TYPE	Bug
	Fighting
ABILITIES	Swarm
	Guts
HEIGHT	4′11″
WEIGHT	119.0 lb.

National Pokédex No.
214

1-
9
50-
99
100-
149
150-
199
200-
249
250-
299
300-
349
350-
399
400-
449
450-
491

Description

Heracross lives in forests, where it feeds off tree sap. Its limbs are very powerful. Rooting its claws in the ground, it can throw its opponents far away with a toss of its horn.

Special Moves

Night Slash, Close Combat, Megahorn

EVO LUT ION

Heracross

Does not Evolve

217

SNEASEL

Pokémon Data

Sharp Claw Pokémon

TYPE	Dark
	Ice
ABILITIES	Inner Focus
	Keen Eye
HEIGHT	2´11˝
WEIGHT	61.7 lb.

Description

Sneasel keeps its claws hidden, extruding them suddenly to slash at an enemy's weak point. It will not stop attacking until its opponent is too weak to move.

National Pokédex No.

215

Special Moves

Fury Swipes, Icy Wind, Taunt, Faint Attack

EVOLUTION

Sneasel → Weavile

TEDDIURSA

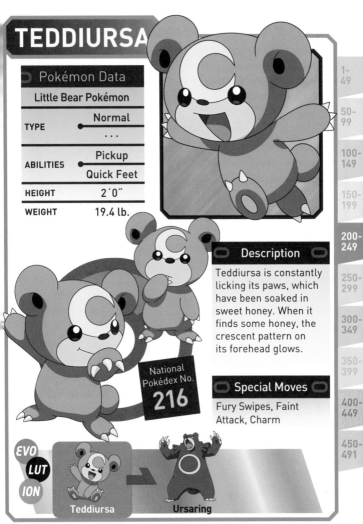

Pokémon Data

Little Bear Pokémon

TYPE	Normal
	. . .
ABILITIES	Pickup
	Quick Feet
HEIGHT	2´0˝
WEIGHT	19.4 lb.

National Pokédex No.
216

Description

Teddiursa is constantly licking its paws, which have been soaked in sweet honey. When it finds some honey, the crescent pattern on its forehead glows.

Special Moves

Fury Swipes, Faint Attack, Charm

EVO LUT ION

Teddiursa → Ursaring

1-49
50-99
100-149
150-199
200-249
250-299
300-349
350-399
400-449
450-491

URSARING

Pokémon Data

Hibernator Pokémon

TYPE	Normal
	. . .
ABILITIES	Guts
	Quick Feet
HEIGHT	5′11″
WEIGHT	277.3 lb.

Description

Ursaring can sniff out food buried deep underground. It leaves claw marks on the trees within its territory that bear the most delicious nuts and fruits.

Special Moves

Scary Face, Hammer Arm, Thrash

National Pokédex No. 217

EVO LUT ION

Teddiursa → Ursaring

SLUGMA

Pokémon Data

Lava Pokémon	
TYPE	Fire
	. . .
ABILITIES	Magma Armor
	Flame Body
HEIGHT	2′4″
WEIGHT	77.2 lb.

National Pokédex No.
218

Description

Slugma's body is made of lava; instead of blood, extremely hot magma runs through its veins. It can't stop moving, or its body will cool off and harden.

Special Moves

Smog, Lava Plume, Ember

1-49
50-99
100-149
150-199
200-249
250-299
300-349
350-399
400-449
450-491

EVO LUT ION

Slugma → Magcargo

MAGCARGO

Pokémon Data

Lava Pokémon

TYPE	Fire
	Rock
ABILITIES	Magma Armor
	Flame Body
HEIGHT	2′7″
WEIGHT	121.3 lb.

Description

Magcargo's shell is created by magma that has cooled and hardened. High-temperature flames burst out from between cracks in the shell.

National Pokédex No.
219

Special Moves

Rock Slide, Body Slam, Flamethrower

EVO
LUT
ION

Slugma → Magcargo

SWINUB

1-
49

50-
99

100-
149

150-
199

200-
249

250-
299

300-
349

350-
399

400-
449

450-
491

Pokémon Data

Pig Pokémon	
TYPE	Ice
	Ground
ABILITIES	Oblivious
	Snow Cloak
HEIGHT	1´4″
WEIGHT	14.3 lb.

National Pokédex No.
220

Description

Swineub loves the mushrooms that grow under dead grass. It will search for them with its nose to the ground, tracking their scent. It also can find hot springs.

Special Moves

Odor Sleuth, Powder Snow, Mud-Slap, Endure

EVO LUT ION

Swinub — Piloswine — Mamoswine

223

PILOSWINE

Pokémon Data

Swine Pokémon

TYPE	Ice
	Ground
ABILITIES	Oblivious
	Snow Cloak
HEIGHT	3′7″
WEIGHT	123.0 lb.

National Pokédex No.
221

Description

Although it can't see well because of the long hair that hangs down over its eyes, Piloswine perceives its surroundings using its sensitive nose. It is also very sensitive to sound.

Special Moves

Powder Snow, Ice Fang, Take Down, Earthquake

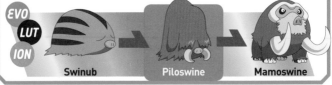

EVO LUT ION

Swinub → Piloswine → Mamoswine

CORSOLA

Pokémon Data

Coral Pokémon	

TYPE	Water
	Rock
ABILITIES	Hustle
	Natural Cure
HEIGHT	2′0″
WEIGHT	11.0 lb.

National Pokédex No.
222

1-49
50-99
100-149
150-199
200-249
250-299
300-349
350-399
400-449
450-491

Description

Many Corsola live in the warm, clean waters of the southern seas. They cannot survive in polluted waters. If one of its spikes is broken off, it can be regrown overnight.

Special Moves

Harden, Rock Blast, Spike Cannon

EVO LUT ION

Corsola

Does not Evolve

REMORAID

Pokémon Data

Jet Pokémon	
TYPE	Water
	. . .
ABILITIES	Hustle
	Sniper
HEIGHT	2´0˝
WEIGHT	26.5 lb.

National Pokédex No.
223

Description

Remoraid shoots down prey by squirting jets of water from its mouth. Its aim is very accurate. It attaches itself to Mantine, feeding off of the larger Pokémon's scraps.

Special Moves

Water Gun, Lock-On, Aurora Beam

EVO LUT ION

Remoraid → Octillery

OCTILLERY

Pokémon Data

Jet Pokémon	
TYPE	Water
	. . .
ABILITIES	Suction Cups
	Sniper
HEIGHT	2′11″
WEIGHT	62.8 lb.

National
Pokédex No.
224

Description

Octillery constructs its nest by digging under rocks and in holes on the sea floor. It confuses its foes by emitting a cloud of murky ink, and catches its prey by snaring it with its arms.

Special Moves

Octazooka, Wring Out, Ice Beam

1–49
50–99
100–149
150–199
200–249
250–299
300–349
350–399
400–449
450–491

EVO LUT ION

Remoraid → Octillery

DELIBIRD

Pokémon Data

Delivery Pokémon

TYPE	Ice
	Flying
ABILITIES	Vital Spirit
	Hustle
HEIGHT	2´11˝
WEIGHT	35.3 lb.

National Pokédex No.
225

Description

Delibird builds its nest on sharp cliffs. It wraps food in its tail, then brings the food to its chicks waiting at the nest. It also shares its food with anyone who's lost in the mountains.

Special Moves

Present

EVO LUT ION

Delibird — Does not Evolve

MANTINE

1-49

50-99

100-149

150-199

200-249

250-299

300-349

350-399

400-449

450-491

Pokémon Data

Kite Pokémon

TYPE	Water
	Flying
ABILITIES	Swift Swim
	Water Absorb
HEIGHT	6´11″
WEIGHT	485.0 lb.

National Pokédex No.
226

Description

Even with Remoraid stuck to it, Mantine easily and swiftly roams the oceans. By building up enough speed, it can jump up out of the waves.

Special Moves

Bounce, Water Pulse, Hydro Pump

EVO LUT ION

Mantyke

Mantine

229

SKARMORY

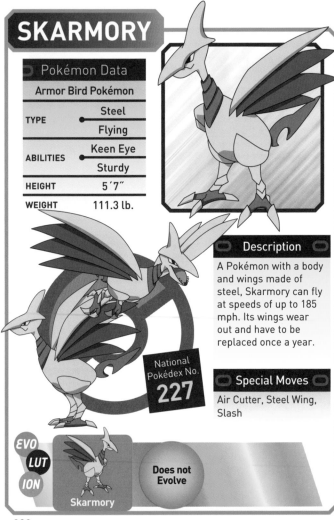

Pokémon Data

Armor Bird Pokémon

TYPE	Steel
	Flying
ABILITIES	Keen Eye
	Sturdy
HEIGHT	5´7˝
WEIGHT	111.3 lb.

Description

A Pokémon with a body and wings made of steel, Skarmory can fly at speeds of up to 185 mph. Its wings wear out and have to be replaced once a year.

National Pokédex No.
227

Special Moves

Air Cutter, Steel Wing, Slash

EVO LUT ION

Skarmory

Does not Evolve

HOUNDOUR

1-49
50-99
100-149
150-199
200-249
250-299
300-349
350-399
400-449
450-491

Pokémon Data

Dark Pokémon

TYPE	Dark
	Fire
ABILITIES	Early Bird
	Flash Fire
HEIGHT	2′0″
WEIGHT	23.8 lb.

National Pokédex No.

228

Description

Houndour communicate with their pack mates using a wide variety of calls, the meaning of which only they can understand. They take down prey by using a tag-team approach.

Special Moves

Howl, Bite, Fire Fang

EVOLUTION

Houndour → Houndoom

HOUNDOOM

Pokémon Data

Dark Pokémon

TYPE	Dark
	Fire
ABILITIES	Early Bird
	Flash Fire
HEIGHT	4'7"
WEIGHT	77.2 lb.

National Pokédex No.
229

Description

After hearing one of Houndoom's eerie howls, most Pokémon get scared and run away. A burn caused by the flames breathed out by Houndoom will almost never heal.

Special Moves

Fire Fang, Crunch, Flamethrower

EVO
LUT
ION

Houndour → Houndoom

KINGDRA

Pokémon Data

Dragon Pokémon	
TYPE	Water
	Dragon
ABILITIES	Swift Swim
	Sniper
HEIGHT	5'11"
WEIGHT	335.1 lb.

National
Pokédex No.
230

Description

Kingdra lives in caves at the bottom of the ocean. Whenever a typhoon comes up it awakens and goes in search of food. When it moves it creates a gigantic whirlpool.

Special Moves

Agility, Dragon Pulse, Brine

1-49
50-99
100-149
150-199
200-249
250-299
300-349
350-399
400-449
450-491

EVO LUT ION

Horsea   Seadra   Kingdra

PHANPY

Pokémon Data

Long Nose Pokémon

TYPE	Ground
	...
ABILITIES	Pickup
	...
HEIGHT	1´8˝
WEIGHT	73.9 lb.

National Pokédex No.
231

Description

Phanpy live in holes dug next to riverbanks. They splash each other with water using their long snouts. Although Phanpy is small it can carry a full-grown human.

Special Moves

Defense Curl, Tackle, Slam

EVO LUT ION

Phanpy

Donphan

DONPHAN

Pokémon Data

Armor Pokémon

TYPE	Ground
	...
ABILITIES	Sturdy
	...
HEIGHT	3'7"
WEIGHT	264.6 lb.

National Pokédex No.
232

1-49

50-99

100-149

150-199

200-249

250-299

300-349

350-399

400-449

450-491

Description

Donphan attacks by rolling up its body and charging straight into its enemy. It puts its strength to good use by helping to remove rockslides that have blocked mountain roads.

Special Moves

Fury Attack, Earthquake, Horn Attack, Rollout

EVO LUT ION

Phanpy

Donphan

PORYGON2

National Pokédex No.

233

Description

An improvement on the original Porygon, Porygon2 was created for experimental space travel use. Occasionally it acts outside of its programming.

Special Moves

Signal Beam, Recycle, Conversion 2

EVO
LUT
ION

Porygon → Porygon2 → Porygon-Z

STANTLER

Pokémon Data

Big Horn Pokémon

TYPE	Normal
	. . .
ABILITIES	Intimidate
	Frisk
HEIGHT	4′7″
WEIGHT	157.0 lb.

National Pokédex No.
234

Description

Staring at its antlers causes the senses to go haywire. This is because the antlers' curvature subtly changes the airflow around them, creating what seems to be a warping of space.

Special Moves

Stomp, Take Down, Zen Headbutt

EVOLUTION

Stantler → Does not Evolve

1-49
50-99
100-149
150-199
200-249
250-299
300-349
350-399
400-449
450-491

SMEARGLE

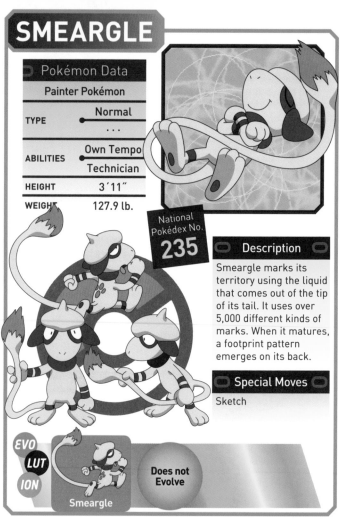

Pokémon Data

Painter Pokémon

TYPE	Normal . . .
ABILITIES	Own Tempo Technician
HEIGHT	3´11˝
WEIGHT	127.9 lb.

National Pokédex No.

235

Description

Smeargle marks its territory using the liquid that comes out of the tip of its tail. It uses over 5,000 different kinds of marks. When it matures, a footprint pattern emerges on its back.

Special Moves

Sketch

EVO LUT ION

Smeargle

Does not Evolve

TYROGUE

1-
49

50-
99

100-
149

150-
199

200-
249

250-
299

300-
349

350-
399

400-
449

450-
491

Pokémon Data

Scuffle Pokémon	
TYPE	Fighting
	. . .
ABILITIES	Guts
	Steadfast
HEIGHT	2´4˝
WEIGHT	46.3 lb.

National
Pokédex No.
236

Description

Known for being quick
to start a fight, Tyrogue
likes to fight against
opponents larger
than itself, and so is
constantly covered
with cuts and bruises.

Special Moves

Tackle, Helping Hand,
Fake Out

EVO LUT ION

Tyrogue   Hitmonchan Hitmontop Hitmonlee

239

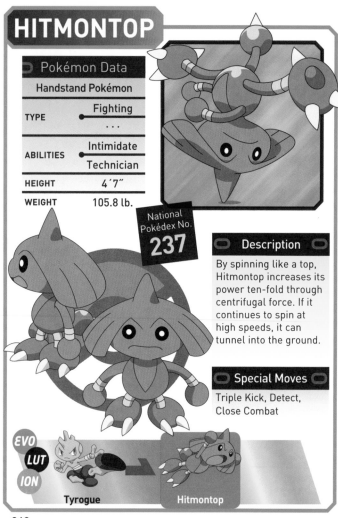

HITMONTOP

Pokémon Data

Handstand Pokémon

TYPE	Fighting · · ·
ABILITIES	Intimidate / Technician
HEIGHT	4´7″
WEIGHT	105.8 lb.

National Pokédex No.
237

Description

By spinning like a top, Hitmontop increases its power ten-fold through centrifugal force. If it continues to spin at high speeds, it can tunnel into the ground.

Special Moves

Triple Kick, Detect, Close Combat

EVOLUTION

Tyrogue → Hitmontop

SMOOCHUM

Pokémon Data

Kiss Pokémon	
TYPE	Ice
	Psychic
ABILITIES	Oblivious
	Forewarn
HEIGHT	1´4˝
WEIGHT	13.2 lb.

1–49

50–99

100–149

150–199

200–249

250–299

300–349

350–399

400–449

450–491

National Pokédex No.
238

Description

Smoochum determines the nature of things by first touching them with its very sensitive lips. It constantly bobs its head back and forth in a kissing motion.

Special Moves

Sweet Kiss, Powder Snow, Confusion

EVO LUT ION

Smoochum → Jynx

ELEKID

Pokémon Data

Electric Pokémon

TYPE	Electric
	...
ABILITIES	Static
	...
HEIGHT	2′0″
WEIGHT	51.8 lb.

National Pokédex No.
239

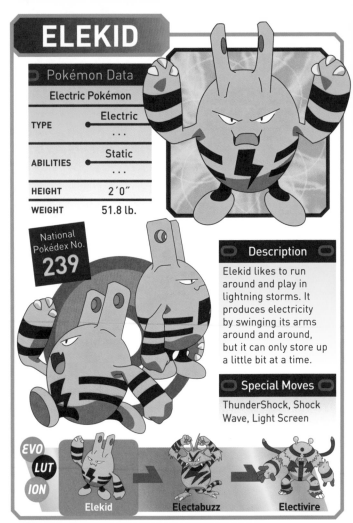

Description

Elekid likes to run around and play in lightning storms. It produces electricity by swinging its arms around and around, but it can only store up a little bit at a time.

Special Moves

ThunderShock, Shock Wave, Light Screen

EVOLUTION

Elekid → Electabuzz → Electivire

MAGBY

Pokémon Data

Live Coal Pokémon

TYPE	Fire . . .
ABILITIES	Flame Body . . .
HEIGHT	2′4″
WEIGHT	47.2 lb.

1–
49

50–
99

100–
149

150–
199

200–
249

250–
299

300–
349

350–
399

400–
449

450–
491

Description

As Magby breathes, fire embers spill from its mouth and nose. When it's happy and energetic, it emits yellow flames. Its internal temperature is over 1,100°F.

Special Moves

Ember, Smokescreen, Smog

National Pokédex No.
240

EVO LUT ION

Magby

Magmar

Magmortar

243

MILTANK

Pokémon Data

Milk Cow Pokémon

TYPE	Normal
	. . .
ABILITIES	Thick Fat
	Scrappy
HEIGHT	3´11˝
WEIGHT	166.4 lb.

National Pokédex No.
241

Description

Milktank's nutrient-rich milk makes children strong and helps sick patients to get better.

Special Moves

Body Slam, Heal Bell, Rollout, Milk Drink

EVO LUT ION

Miltank

Does not Evolve

BLISSEY

Pokémon Data

Happiness Pokémon

TYPE
Normal
. . .

ABILITIES
Natural Cure
Serene Grace

HEIGHT 4´11˝

WEIGHT 103.2 lb.

National Pokédex No.
242

1-49
50-
300-149
150-199
200-249
250-299
300-349
350-399
400-449
450-491

Description

Blissey is a Pokémon that brings happiness. It nurses weakened Pokémon until they are better. It has a very gentle personality.

Special Moves

Sing, Egg Bomb, Healing Wish

EVO LUT ION

Happiny ➤ Chansey ➤ Blissey

RAIKOU

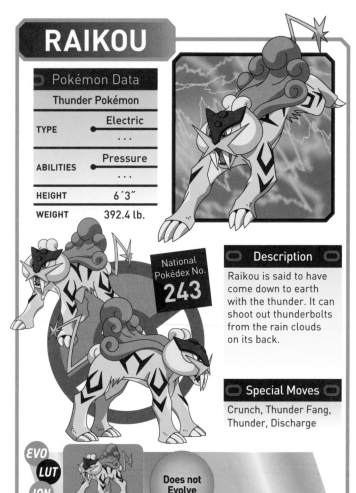

Pokémon Data

Thunder Pokémon

TYPE	Electric ...
ABILITIES	Pressure ...
HEIGHT	6′3″
WEIGHT	392.4 lb.

National Pokédex No.
243

Description

Raikou is said to have come down to earth with the thunder. It can shoot out thunderbolts from the rain clouds on its back.

Special Moves

Crunch, Thunder Fang, Thunder, Discharge

EVO LUT ION

Raikou

Does not Evolve

ENTEI

Pokémon Data

Volcano Pokémon

TYPE
Fire
...

ABILITIES
Pressure
...

HEIGHT 6'11"

WEIGHT 436.5 lb.

Description

Another Entei is born whenever a new volcano is created, and it is said that when Entei roars, somewhere a volcano erupts. It roams all over the world.

Special Moves

Flamethrower, Fire Fang, Fire Blast

National Pokédex No.
244

EVOLUTION

Entei

Does not Evolve

1–49
50–99
100–149
150–199
200–249
250–299
300–349
350–399
400–449
450–491

SUICUNE

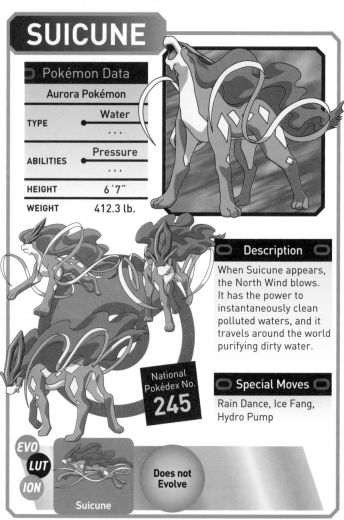

Pokémon Data

Aurora Pokémon

TYPE	Water . . .
ABILITIES	Pressure . . .
HEIGHT	6´7˝
WEIGHT	412.3 lb.

Description

When Suicune appears, the North Wind blows. It has the power to instantaneously clean polluted waters, and it travels around the world purifying dirty water.

National Pokédex No.
245

Special Moves

Rain Dance, Ice Fang, Hydro Pump

EVO
LUT
ION

Suicune

Does not Evolve

Take a trip with Pokémon

ALL THAT PIKACHU!
ANI-MANGA

Meet Pikachu and all-star Pokémon! Two complete Pikachu stories taken from the Pokémon movies—all in a full color manga.

Buy yours today at store.viz.com!

Pokémon
www.pokemon.com

vizkids

www.viz.com

**The Complete Pokémon Pocket Guide
Volume 1
VIZ Kids Edition**

© 2008 Pokémon.
© 1995–2008 Nintendo/Creatures Inc./GAME FREAK inc.
TM and ® and character names are trademarks of Nintendo.
© 2007 Jungle Factory/Shogakukan
All rights reserved.
Original Japanese edition "Pokémon DIAMOND PEARL
ZENKOKU ZENKYARA DAIZUKAN JOU"
published by SHOGAKUKAN Inc.

Translation/Kaori Inoue
Interior Design/Courtney Utt, Bustah Brown Design Inc., Hidemi Sahara
Cover Design/Hitomi Yokoyama Ross
Editor/Leyla Aker

Printed in Singapore

Published by VIZ Media, LLC
P.O. Box 77010
San Francisco, CA 94107

10 9 8 7 6 5
First printing, October 2008
Fifth printing, January 2012

www.vizkids.com

THE COMPLETE POKÉMON POCKET GUIDE

#001-245 Bulbasaur to Suicune

1